WHO IS
PHOEBE BUTTANSHAW?

Jane Quinn

PHOENIX PRESS LTD

Published 2023
First Edition
Phoenix Press Ltd
www.newhavenpublishingltd.com
newhavenpublishing@gmail.com

Cover Design © Holly Bushnell

Content

DON'T WORRY BEE HAPPY
Kip O'Conner as King Arthur
Me mowing the O'Conner's lawn
Augie - the world's GREATEST dog
Cricket Alison - Annie's surgeon
RAINBOWS ONLY FOLLOW STORMS
LOVE + PEACE
Aunt Sue's birthday present
Me & Kip
Love is all you need

Meet Phoebe

Phoebe Buttanshaw was shy. She wasn't shy in a pretty, princess way with flirtatious eyes and a pale pink blush. Phoebe Buttanshaw was shy in an all-out, eyes-glued-to-the-ground sort of way; and when Phoebe blushed it was an all-over, crimson sort of blush. At the age of 13, she was old enough to be aware of shyness, but Phoebe had just learned to live with its presence. It seemed to invade her as if it were not a part of her at all but some alien force enveloping her at the most inconvenient times.

For example, there was that time at Petland. She'd been mowing lawns to earn extra pocket money and decided to research the possibilities of pet ownership. Phoebe loved animals, and they loved her. Animals never seemed to say rude things about Phoebe's glasses or freckles. It had occurred to her that it was almost as if they took no notice of such things at all, and Phoebe liked that. So, on that hot July day, Phoebe set off to visit Petland.

Mr Dutton was the proprietor of Petland and had been the proprietor longer than Phoebe had been alive. Mr Dutton had a face that Phoebe had seen on a certain dog famous for his appearances on television advertisements. Phoebe had a difficult time making eye contact with most people even on her best days, but it was especially challenging to be face to face with a blubbering bulldog; so Phoebe usually made quick, inconspicuous visits to the puppy play area and the aquarium avoiding Mr Dutton lest she collapse in a giggling, blushing mass of embarrassment.

Today she decided to conquer the obstacles – the giggle attacks and the shyness thing (which Phoebe had come to know simply as "the thing") in pursuit of a much more urgent and important endeavour. Phoebe Buttanshaw was going to meet her very own new friend. Would it be a cat? A lop-eared rabbit? (Phoebe adored lop-eared rabbits, all soft and dewy-eyed.) A longhaired guinea pig? It was going to be a superlative day!

Phoebe pushed open the door that marked the magical entrance to Mr Dutton's Petland. She adjusted her round spectacles and felt a smile infiltrate her entire being. And then it happened. A voice asked, "May I help you?" But it wasn't the voice of a bulldog. Curious, Phoebe turned quickly around and found that the voice, in fact, belonged to a boy. He was a little older than Phoebe with dark curls that fell onto his forehead in just the right way. His official red Petland blazer sported a large, circular badge which seemed to shout, "I'm Kip and this is Petland!" Direct and to the point, Phoebe thought in that split second before she felt her flaying arms crash into the mile-high display of dog food tins.

The resulting catastrophe caused a major invasion by "the thing" complete with crimson cheeks, hot flashes, and eyes that not only searched the floor but actually filled with tears unlike any that Phoebe had shed since that afternoon she accompanied her eager parents to the re-release of Walt Disney's Bambi. They loved it. Phoebe hated it – too, too sad for her with that heartbroken little deer.

And so ended Phoebe Buttanshaw's long-awaited visit to Mr Dutton's Petland. But that was weeks ago. In the meantime, Phoebe continued mowing lawns in those grass-stained plimsolls with the missing toes and broken laces. She was no longer sure of exactly why she mowed the lawns. She knew that she would never again go into Petland, so the money she was earning had somehow lost all significance.

Instead Phoebe mowed because when she mowed she could become part of the out-of-doors. She could smell that wonderful clean fragrance of newly mown grass, and she felt sorrow for the nomads of the faraway deserts where such an aroma was unknown. She watched all the birds of all the trees as they chattered and made plans for their next migration. The occasional rabbit might magically appear and disappear, lifting Phoebe's spirits to new heights. And so the summer went.

It was September, and Phoebe had all but forgotten the Petland incident – well, except for the occasional nightmare when she would relive the fiasco in slow motion and, for some unexplained reason, wearing roller skates!

School would soon reclaim Phoebe Buttanshaw, and she would leave her lawns behind to return to her books. She would exchange what was left of the canvas plimsolls for a pair of sensible, black lace-ups with appropriate grey woolly knee socks. But first Phoebe had to mow the lawn of the O'Conner family.

They were new in Phoebe's neighbourhood, having moved in unnoticed sometime during the summer. Mrs O'Conner met Mrs Buttanshaw at the library where they both volunteered their services one afternoon each week. Mrs O'Conner mentioned what a chore it was to keep the lawn mowed what with all the rain we'd been having and Mr O'Conner travelling so much in his new job, and now her teenage son had taken a summer job leaving the lawn to its own devices. That was when Mrs Buttanshaw mentioned that she had a daughter who was a whiz at converting out-of-control grasslands into dream gardens.

And so it was arranged that Phoebe would have a go at the O'Conner's back lawn on Friday. She welcomed the chance to get to know a new patch of green and to meet its tenants. She wondered if there might be an O'Conner rabbit lurking about.

No one appeared to be at home when Phoebe entered the awaiting O'Conner garden that Friday morning. That was okay, though, because when Phoebe met new people "the thing" usually tried to butt in anyway. She was quite content to set about her business in solitude.

As she walked around the perimeter of the garden for the first time, Phoebe's thoughts were with her feet. The shoelaces on the green plimsolls were both missing now because there were just too many knots in them to fit through the holes, and the left sole had given up its fight to hold on. Phoebe was wondering if the familiar old shoes could survive this last week of the summer holiday when she heard a friendly greeting from a friendly dog. Oh, Phoebe did enjoy meeting friendly dogs. She'd longed for a dog of her own for years but had never quite convinced the elder Buttanshaws who never seemed to come up with any original arguments against inviting a dog into the family. It was always the same. What happens when we go on holiday? The garden is too small. There would be hair on the sofa! Phoebe became exasperated when she thought of it, so she took this surprise opportunity to give this friendly creature a good scratch and pet.

He was smallish but not in that too small way that some dogs have about them. He had a good pink tongue that licked at her hand as she reached for him. His hair was coarse and defied description as well as the comb, she thought. It was every colour – silver, brown, black, blonde. She wondered what his name was as he danced with the purest of joy known only to young dogs. This, Phoebe concluded at once, was a truly splendid dog.

It was a long time before Phoebe could take serious notice of the job which stretched out before her. She was far too busy dancing around the garden with the nameless, brindle dog until she suddenly felt a presence nearby. Was someone watching from a window? There didn't appear to be any faces in the many windows of the O'Conner house. Was someone at the gate? Again the answer was no. It was then she felt the eyes upon her more strongly than ever. Above me, she thought. Yes, there, all but hidden in the leafy green, were two brown eyes fixed on Phoebe and the brindle dog. She looked harder and saw a mop of dark curls just above those brown eyes.

"Got anything to sharpen a pencil with?" A voice came from the tree. "I'm…" But Phoebe already knew. The image of the great, round badge against the red blazer was etched forever in her memory.

Oh no, Phoebe thought. "The thing" wasted no time in moving in. Phoebe didn't seem to be able to move. And why would she have a pencil sharpener anyway, and why would a boy in a tree need one? Disjointed thoughts rushed through Phoebe's mind, but she didn't speak. She didn't move. She just blushed.

"Hot day, huh?" said the voice from the tree. Phoebe had no doubt that he was trying to make a polite excuse for her red cheeks, but still she did not speak. Funnily, however, she found that her eyes didn't automatically drop to the ground as normally happened at such times. Instead they were fixed on the green leaves where a moment before she had spotted the curls. Phoebe was curious. Was the curiosity fighting back "the thing?" Hmmm....she wondered.

"Augie!" shouted the voice suddenly and loudly and – well – curiously. Phoebe wondered just what that could mean. She soon found out.

There he was! The boy with the perfectly, imperfect curls and the Petland badge and – what was that? – a pencil in his hand! He flew from the branches, landing magnificently on his feet. Again he shouted, "Augie," but before Phoebe could catch her breath he was off in full chase. She turned in time to see the bottom of the brindle dog squeeze through a broken board in the fence at the far end of the garden. The race was on. Phoebe watched as the blur of brindle disappeared followed by the blur of a red Petland blazer. She decided to join in; and as she did, she wished with all her might that she'd worn better shoes!

The small dog seemed to find his stubby legs no handicap as he headed down a path that must have been a familiar one to him. He dodged cars, jumped over obstacles, and ignored the distraction of neighbourhood cats until finally he entered the gates of Ripple Park where he perched atop a fallen log and waited knowingly for the pair who were certain to arrive.

Kip had made his appearance and was giving the dog a fine telling off by the time that Phoebe limped in with both soles now flapping. The disintegration of her shoes plus the sudden fogging of her glasses made the last few yards of her journey difficult ones. As she approached the very cross boy and his very pleased dog, Phoebe thought that they were a very funny pair. She could see in the boy's annoyed, brown eyes a real tenderness for that messy, disobedient dog; but, more than that, she could see the same affection in the eyes of the runaway. Here was something that Phoebe could understand. That is when the two became three, and there wasn't a sign of "the thing" anywhere.

Maybe Phoebe had outrun it in the chase, in spite of her footwear; or maybe it just didn't seem important anymore. She never really found out where "the thing" went. She was just happy that it was anywhere other than in Ripple Park on that Friday afternoon.

Phoebe Meets Kip and Augie

"What kind of name is Augie anyway?" Phoebe and Kip and the brindle dog walked through the wildest parts of Ripple Park as the afternoon wore on. Kip just couldn't deny his furry friend a good run even though he'd felt very angry with him earlier.

"Short for Augustus which means August," Kip explained in a rhythm that hinted that he'd told the story a few times before. "Augie didn't like the name Augustus so I shortened it to Augie. He seems happy with it. At least he answers to it – when he wants to."

Phoebe's remaining shreds of canvas were now being carried in her hands rather than worn upon her feet. "Oh," she suddenly got the connection. "He was born in August?"

"Mo, September…"

"Oh," Phoebe accepted his logic or lack of logic without question. She liked Kip and Augie. They were funny and different and yet, somehow, she thought, very much like her. She learned a lot about them as they walked and talked. Kip was nearly 15 – well, he was 14 and a bit. He was also the cleverest writer of wit and sketcher of whimsy ever! Phoebe drew this conclusion from the way he spoke and the bits of paper in his pockets which were covered in doodles, but mostly she knew because Kip told her.

His confidence bubbled out of every inch of him so Phoebe found herself agreeing that it must be true, and she decided right then and there that if anyone she knew was ever to become famous that it would be Kip O'Conner.

She was just feeling very lucky to have been standing under that tree when Kip had fallen from it when, suddenly, Phoebe remembered why she'd been under that tree. The lawn!

The race was on again as the three ran all the way back to the rear gate of the O'Conner garden. On the way, Phoebe threw what was left of the old plimsolls into a rubbish bin and tried to ignore the stones bruising her bare feet.

As Kip pushed open the gate they could see a plainly unamused Mrs O'Conner looking up and down the length of the garden hoping for a sign that some patch of grass somewhere had been mown. Phoebe Buttanshaw had never let a customer down before. She'd never let one of her mother's friends down before. Actually, Phoebe had never let anyone down before, and she found herself feeling sick at the prospect of explaining her momentary lapse of responsibility to Mrs O'Conner. Her brain seemed to freeze as her mouth refused to open at all. The walk up the garden path seemed unending. Was she trying to climb up the down escalator, she wondered? Surely Mrs O'Conner must be wondering why this red-faced, sweaty girl with bare feet and steamy glasses was having such a difficult time walking towards her.

Of course, Phoebe did eventually come within inches of the steely Mrs O'Conner, but that's when things took a dramatic turn of events.

Before Phoebe could encourage her jaws to get into gear, Kip swept between her and his mother. Phoebe heard his words, but he seemed to be speaking of other people and other places. A dream perhaps. She couldn't quite get the connection between what Kip was saying and what had transpired on this day.

Mrs O'Conner's eyes suddenly lit up, her face softened, and she even smiled as Kip related the adventure. According to him, Phoebe had just arrived with her lawnmower – precisely at 1:00 as arranged – when a big, white van pulled up. What must have been a dozen frantic men and women climbed out. Kip said it was particularly funny because it reminded him of a dozen circus clowns squashed into a tiny peddle car. Phoebe found herself enthralled.

Kip said that the mystery visitors identified themselves as a television film crew in search of an overgrown garden to use as a backdrop for the scene they were scheduled to shoot that very afternoon. It was to be part of a tv drama about a band of marauding children who lived wild and free beneath tangled tree roots and grass gone to seed. They couldn't believe their luck when they drove, purely by chance, past this jungle of a garden. Naturally, Kip volunteered the use of the garden, seeing it as far more important than Phoebe's chore of mowing the grass.

"Oh, yes, Kip. Yes, indeed. Wonderful." Mrs O'Conner wanted more details. "When will we see our garden on television? When?"

"Oh, not exactly sure. You know how scheduling can be – such a bore. I'll just keep an eye on the listings." Kip never missed a beat.

By now Phoebe knew that her jaws were once again in working order because her mouth had dropped open very wide. She looked at Kip and then at Mrs O'Conner. They were both extremely pleased with the story. Phoebe even looked to Augie, hoping for some explanation, but he'd fallen fast asleep under the last remaining sunlight of the day. Was she going mad? Or perhaps she really had been part of a television film but had forgotten all about it. Or – just maybe – she'd learned something rather startling about her creative friend. It would appear that his stories didn't contain themselves to the written page. They seemed instead to jump right out of his head and into real life.

Phoebe collected her belongings and started towards the garden gate, the very same gate that she had walked through so many times already that day. She said her farewells, promising to be back the next day to spruce up the lawn; and then she walked home, wondering what exactly had happened to her that day.

Phoebe Starts School

Phoebe Buttanshaw was not what her mother would refer to as a "petite" girl. She was, in fact, the tallest girl in her class at school just as she had been since the age of 5 when she began her academic life at Fielder's Primary School. Mrs Buttanshaw had always been eager to point out Phoebe's size to anyone who would listen – sales assistants, other mothers, the girl behind the deli counter.

Most girls of Phoebe's age seemed to love shopping for clothes, but Phoebe's recollections of such excursions were of the shatteringly loud observations made by girls paid to make light conversation with prospective customers.

"Why, she's very BIG for her age, isn't she?"

"Maybe you should try the Big & Tall Girl's Department."

Once when Phoebe was 9 or 10 years old and had just discovered the delights of double cheeseburger and deepest pan pizza with extra cheese, she was actually referred to the Chubettes Department at the local clothing shop. It was, claimed the sales clerk, for "special" girls who had "special" needs in clothing. Phoebe knew exactly what it was. She also knew that all the Buttanshaws were of generous proportions. She had always thought that that must be to house their generous personalities, but just on rare occasion Phoebe couldn't help but be a tiny bit envious of those of smaller embodiments.

Actually, it was just one smaller embodiment that sparked this strange feeling. It was, and always had been, Cricket Allison. Cricket was about the same age as Phoebe, and they both lived on Elm Road, and they had both attended Fielder's School since that very first day when they were 5 years old. Phoebe remembered it as if it were yesterday.

She had awakened earlier than usual and earlier than necessary felling excited, fearful, happy, sad, unsure but expectant, and – yes – very shy. She'd been a confused mass of near-hysteria as she walked up the steps of the ancient building for the very first time. The belfry seemed to rise up and up into the sky without ever really having a visible ending. It reminded Phoebe of Jack's beanstalk, and she came to a standstill at the prospect of giants lurking around corners. All other apprehensions were pushed from her mind, and that was when it happened. With her head tipped back as far as it could go so that she might see any bats making their escape from the belfry, Phoebe's new straw hat tumbled straight off the back of her head and under the tiniest feet of the tiniest girl that she'd seen amongst this group of newer-than-new students.

The small girl stepped on the hat over and over. She seemed to be doing a mad version of the Mexican hat dance or perhaps she'd slipped over the edge, what with all the excitement, and just couldn't control her dainty little feet. There had to be a logical explanation, Phoebe reasoned. Why would a complete stranger want to destroy her new hat if she wasn't deranged or dancing? The little girl smiled a small, dainty smile and skipped up the steps while Phoebe was left to collect the bits of torn straw.

Once inside the classroom, Phoebe took the opportunity to survey all the strange decorations, posters, and pictures hung on every wall. There were colourful cutouts of umbrellas and paper cats and drawings depicting the months of the year. And written in very large, very simple letters on the whiteboard was "Miss Boat." Phoebe knew what the letters said because she'd figured out this mystery called reading ages ago. She could read the letters and sound out most words and wasn't too bad at writing her name either. She thought that she would do okay at school if only people would stop stepping on her hat.

The tall, skinny lady who walked into the classroom announced that she was, in fact, the very same Miss Boat whose name appeared on the board. She looked pretty scary on first sight, but Phoebe was a fair girl who planned to give her every chance. But then Miss Boat did something which Phoebe later discovered would become routine throughout her years at Fielder's. She looked at the nervous little faces and said, "Now, I want you to line up according to your height." As she spoke, Miss Boat walked up to Phoebe and pulled her from the crowd. "My, you are a big girl, aren't you? You will no doubt go to the end of our line."

Phoebe was bright red and not at all happy with all the little eyes staring at her. One by one the others were examined and placed here or there.

In the end, Phoebe was the final student in the long row of 5 year olds exactly as Miss Boat had predicted. Phoebe lifted her eyes just long enough to glance at her fellow students. At the very front of the line she saw her! She couldn't believe it. She'd been hoping desperately that she'd only been someone's baby sister; but, no, she was definitely in Phoebe's very own classroom!

It was the small girl with unpleasant feet. Miss Boat asked the children to call out their names starting, as always, at the front – or small – end of the line. It was a clear, confident voice that plainly said, "Cricket Allison."

Phoebe didn't take notice of most of the other names. Her attention remained with Cricket Allison. Phoebe had always longed for a cute name rather than her substantial, rather old-fashioned name.

"Phoebe Buttanshaw….Cricket Allison," Phoebe said the words to herself over and over until it was finally her turn to call out her own name. Caught off-guard, she found herself saying, "Crikey – I mean, Phoebe Buttanshaw."

The giggles overtook student after student in a domino effect until Miss Boat had to tap her foot soundly and demand restraint. Shortly, the laughter subsided except for one tinkling giggle plainly coming from the far end of the human chain. Cricket Allison seemed to enjoy Phoebe's slip-up more than was normal to enjoy such a thing.

Phoebe found herself wishing for the first of many times that Cricket Allison would just go away, disappear, or – at the very least – move far away from Elm Road and Fielder-s School. But it wasn't to be. Cricket always seemed to turn up exactly where Phoebe hoped she wouldn't. Like the time that Phoebe's mother enrolled her in a ballet class to hep her to acquire grace. Sure enough, there was little Cricket Allison dancing her heart out in perfect petite form. Or the time that Phoebe had to have two teeth removed to make room for her grown-up teeth. If ever there was a time that Phoebe did not wish to see Cricket or to be seen by Cricket, it was in that dentist's waiting room where she sat fighting off floods of tears and waves of nerve attacks. As Phoebe waited her turn, who should emerge from the dreaded door but a beaming Cricket Allison – all smiles and no cavities!

And so now it was eight years later and Phoebe found herself ready to embark on yet another first day of yet another new school year. The pavements seemed to be full of nothing but new school uniforms and the sound of squeaky, new practical shoes which infiltrated every conversation amongst those returning to Fielder's High School.

Fielder's High School was practically next door to Fielder's Primary School, and both schools were just three streets away from Elm Road.

As usual, Phoebe was ready far too early for her first day at school so she decided to take the scenic route to Fielder's/ That meant walking past the O'Conner house so it would be convenient for Phoebe to call in to see if Kip knew his way to his new school. It was perfect logic, she thought; and, anyway, she hadn't seen Kip or Augie since their adventure in Ripple Park two weeks earlier.

Phoebe wasn't exactly sure why it should be, but this year the start of the school year didn't fill her with dread. In fact, she actually felt happy as she turned into Hillcrest Avenue with a spring in each step that took her toward Kip O'Conner's house.

Phoebe rang the bell and then pushed her glasses up and fluffed her hair. The door opened to reveal Mrs O'Conner. Phoebe couldn't catch her breath at first as thoughts of Kip's fabricated tale of filmmaking in the O'Conner garden raced through her mind. Surely, this seemingly intelligent woman had by now seen the story for what it was and would lash out at Phoebe, accusing her of being a wicked, dishonest girl. Phoebe awaited the verbal assault, but instead Mrs O'Conner smiled at her.

"Oh, Phoebe Buttanshaw. I'm afraid you've missed Kip. He just left for school, but I'm sure you'll catch up with him if you hurry."

Phoebe just managed a 'thank you' and turned in the direction of the school. She was a fast runner, what with her long legs and proper shoes complete with laces and soles. Phoebe felt as if she were on wings as she raced along, but then something quite unexpected happened. Phoebe caught sight of Kip's curls and new Fielder's blazer but – no! – bobbing alongside him was a small figure, a full head shorter than the boy. It couldn't be. But, of course, it was. Cricket Allison, who had always had a knack for being where Phoebe wished she wouldn't be, was now in the very worst place imaginable – by Kip's side.

What a way to start out the new year, Phoebe thought, as she slowed her pace and turned into a quiet pathway. She would take her time getting to Fielder's. After all, there was no reason to rush…no reason at all.

Phoebe's Haircut

Phoebe Buttanshaw had a feeling of impending disaster. Phoebe was famous for her feelings of impending disasters. So far, however, no famine or plagues had visited the Buttanshaw domain.

Dragging herself warily from her bed, Phoebe glanced sideways in the mirror. It was a silly mirror, she thought, with carved clowns cavorting around the frame wearing bright pink and yellow hats. The mirror had hung in that very spot for 13 years, a gift from Phoebe's Aunt Sue on the morning of her birth.

Most days over the past 13 years had begun in the same way for Phoebe – a hurried look at her face reflected back between the peeling pink and yellow paint of the clowns' hats. When Phoebe was an infant, Mrs Buttanshaw used to bounce her about in front of the mirror as she made those silly sounds familiar to any baby whose path has ever crossed that of an adult person's. Then, as a terrible toddler, Phoebe used to pull open all the drawers on her chest of drawers and climb up them, as one would climb a ladder, so that she could stand tall in front of the silly mirror making appropriately silly faces. By the age of six, Phoebe got tremendous joy from jumping on her bed as if it were a circus trampoline. If she jumped really had and bounced really high, she found herself face to face with the Phoebe in the clown mirror. It was great fun.

Around the age of 12, however, something changed. Phoebe no longer sought out her image in the old familiar ways. She avoided her reflection in glass-fronted shops. She disliked those big mirror covered walls in chain store fitting rooms, but most of all she stayed away from the dreaded clown mirror. And now, at age 13, Phoebe ignored the mirror almost completely. She had pretended for so long that it didn't exist that now she rarely noticed it on her wall at all – except for that morning when she awoke with "the feeling."

That wary sideways glance into the clowns really couldn't have been too revealing to Phoebe because she hadn't yet put on her glasses. Still, the blurred image that caught her eye seemed to shout, "Phoebe Buttanshaw, for goodness sake, get a haircut!"

Phoebe grabbed her glasses and stood very close to the girl in the mirror. Yes, she must cut her hair. This revelation came as a bit of a shock to Phoebe because she had spent the entire duration of her 13 years in pursuit of perfect, waist-length hair. Of course, she'd never managed it. She had that kind of hair that was neither very long nor very short. It was neither curly nor straight, and it was neither blonde nor brown. Phoebe suddenly saw it quite plainly as nondescript and boring, and those were two words, which did not appeal to her. The decision had been made. Phoebe Buttanshaw would change her image.

It was over breakfast that Phoebe announced her decision. She would cut her hair into a very short and very pixyish style. Suddenly, she thought, she would appear very waiflike and vulnerable while, at the same time, appearing brave and intriguing. That was what she definitely planned to do.

A moment later Phoebe's plans took a nosedive when Mrs Buttanshaw looked at Phoebe's head from every angle, giving great attention to the forehead, nose, and chin.

"Oh no, dear," Mrs Buttanshaw finally spoke after her lengthy inspection. "You're far too big-boned for a pixie cut. Short haircuts only suit petite girls with small faces. You know, like Mrs Allison's little girl…. Why, she looks darling with her pixie cut; but, Phoebe, honestly, you'd look like a big, clumsy boy. No, no, no. Out of the question."

Phoebe had not heard herself referred to as a little girl since she was seven years old. Yet, here was her own mother speaking of Mrs Allison's little girl who was, at 14, nearly a full year older than Phoebe. These thoughts turned slowly over in her mind until a much more startling thought pushed them aside.

"I don't want Cricket Allison's haircut!" Phoebe shouted silently. Whatever had she been thinking or not thinking? Surely, if she'd actually considered that thought seriously for one minute, she'd have rejected the entire notion immediately.

Cricket had sported variations of the short pixie cut as long as Phoebe had known her, but the image of 'Mrs Allison's little girl' had eluded her on that morning until Mrs Buttanshaw's remarks.

And so that was the end of Phoebe's immediate longing for an elfin haircut; but not, she vowed to herself, for a shake-up in her image. Whatever had she been thinking?

Phoebe had so much to consider on her walk to Fielder's that morning. There was her new look to invent, of course, as well as the impending disaster which she was sure would still arrive.

Entering through the old oak doors of her school, Phoebe looked cautiously over her shoulder, checking for the disaster. All she saw was a gigantic poster announcing the autumn dance. Her eyes did not rest long on the poster. Phoebe had given up dancing long ago – about the time that Cricket Allison became the darling of her ballet class, although she was sure that there was no connection.

And so Phoebe gave no further thought to the event until lunchtime when the subject seemed to be on everyone's lips. They all seemed far more aware about such things as dances this term. She puzzled over this new development for some time while her soggy mashed potatoes took on the texture of cold glue. When she finally stood up to leave her table, from the corner of her eye, Phoebe caught a glimpse of two figures seated at the far end of the room. One was Kip O'Conner, she was certain, although her shortsighted eyes had been known to deceive her on occasion. Yes, it must be him. She'd never known a boy with such lovely curls before, and she could easily identify those curls long before she could make out the face lying beneath them.

Kip had really found a niche for himself at Fielder's High School. Although he'd been there only a matter of weeks, he'd entered easily into the intricate social structure so much a part of any teenage domain. The school magazine boasted the name of Kip O'Conner as assistant editor although Phoebe knew for certain that he would very soon be editor-in-chief. The drama society made no secret of the fact that Kip was their star find. Plans for the first play of the year would soon be underway, and Phoebe's intuition told her that Kip would be centre stage when the curtain rose. She was totally convinced that there was nothing that Kip O'Conner couldn't do.

Phoebe tried to walk nonchalantly from the school lunchroom. She kept her eyes on her feet as she shuffled toward the door. That's when the feeling of dread returned, and she caught a split second look at the figure next to Kip's. Of course, she thought, who else could it be? It was Cricket Allison, and suddenly it all fit together like a neat, little jigsaw. Phoebe saw the two enjoying their lunch together. She saw the poster looming over their heads proclaiming the approach of the first big social happening of the year, and she saw all too clearly and cruelly what form the impending disaster would take. She didn't need to be told, nor would she wait to be told. She just simply knew. Kip O'Conner would be escorting Cricket Allison to the Autumn Ball at Fielder's High School in two weeks' time. There was no doubt in Phoebe's mind.

The following week found Phoebe keeping her mind firmly on such things as schoolwork and hair. She decided to become a dedicated academic who saw no attraction in such frivolities as dances and social gathering. She also decided that she really must get a new hairstyle…and not one remotely like a pixie haircut. And so her week glided by. There was no consideration given to the possibility that Phoebe, herself, might attend the Autumn Ball. Neither did she enter into the inevitable chatter amongst her peers about who would be in attendance with whom. Phoebe knew all she wanted to know about this dance. Kip and Cricket would be there together – dancing together. That was all that Phoebe could see when she thought of the dance, and so she simply did not think of it.

Midway through the second week, the male auditions for the drama society's first play were held. 'Camelot' was the chosen vehicle, and Kip O'Conner was the chosen King Arthur. Phoebe expressed no surprise upon the announcement. She knew that there was nothing out of reach for this new boy with the laughing eyes and unruly curls. The auditions for female cast members would take place the following Wednesday afternoon.

And so it finally came to be Saturday. Phoebe had resigned herself to it. She knew it was to be, and she could not change it. This thing was going to happen. She watched the clock. It was 5:00. Phoebe's imagination told her that Cricket Allison would, at this very moment, be preparing for the ball. Kip was most likely at the florist collecting a carefully selected corsage. Would he pin it onto Cricket's gown? Most boys wouldn't know how, but Kip could do anything.

Phoebe decided at that moment to banish such thoughts from her mind and take action on something within her control. She opened the antique pine box on her chest of drawers, which was just below the clown mirror. She pulled out some of the money she'd earned mowing lawns last summer, which suddenly seemed so very long ago.

Pulling on her warm tweed coat and long red scarf, Phoebe left the Buttanshaw home and ran toward Fandangles, the new unisex hairdresser's that had recently opened just past Ripple Park. Would she get her hair bobbed or feathered or layered or permed? All she knew for certain was that she would soon be a different Phoebe Buttanshaw. Why, maybe she would even get contact lenses soon! Change was definitely in the air!

To get to Fandangles, Phoebe had to walk past the big iron gates of Ripple Park, and Phoebe loved Ripple Park. Maybe, she thought, she'd just have a peek inside to see if any deer were around. She slipped through the gates and walked towards the hill where all the rabbits made their home. She saw movement around the rabbits' holes. What a big rabbit, she thought, with a rush of excitement. She had to get closer. She moved quietly and cautiously so as not to frighten the mysterious animal. And then, suddenly, Phoebe recognised him – Augie! She laughed out loud, surprising herself, as Augie ran from burrow to burrow, teased by the bobbing up and down of rabbits' heads.

"Augie, you bad boy! Come here!" Augie danced up to Phoebe, happy to see her after so long an absence. "If you've run away again, you'll be in terrible trouble. Come on and I'll walk you home."

But as Phoebe turned toward the gates of Ripple Park, she knew that she wouldn't have to return Augie to his master after all. His master was right there perched on top of the big, hollow uprooted trunk of a fallen oak tree. Phoebe was startled…….and puzzled.

"It's cold. What are you doing in the park?" Kip seemed equally surprised to see Phoebe.

"Oh, hair. I mean I'm on my way to get my hair feathered, uh, bobbed, er, I mean cut. I thought you'd be at the dance."

Kip chuckled and looked straight into Phoebe's round glasses. "I like your hair as it is, and the dance didn't appeal really. Besides," he paused. "I can't dance."

And so Phoebe and Kip walked Augie back to Hillcrest Avenue. Afterwards, Phoebe returned home, thinking to herself in amazement, 'Kip can't dance?'

From then on, Phoebe tried to always keep her imagination firmly in check although success eluded her in that area. Oh, yes. Phoebe Buttanshaw never did get that new haircut.

Rag Doll

Phoebe Buttanshaw was thirteen and a half years old and still slept with her one-eyed rag doll who had the name of Annie. At various times Annie had been not only one-eyed but also one-armed, one-legged, and very nearly heartless when ten years ago she'd been dragged around Uncle David's farm and was caught off guard by a protruding, rusty nail in the barn door. A three year-old Phoebe rescued the impaled Annie, and together they flew to Auntie Sue's kitchen where emergency surgery was successful in repairing the torn body of a lifetime friend. Annie still carried the scars across the heart drawn in a child's hand across her white chest.

Phoebe loved Annie; and it was understood that, although she'd never actually found the words, Annie returned the love. The two had shared everything as long as Phoebe could remember – a room, secrets, fears, sleepless nights, and ambitions unknown to those abiding outside the walls of that special room.

And so it was, deep into that October night, that Phoebe pulled Annie very near to her face and whispered into the red yarn hair where an ear would be had she been so blessed. "I am going to be Guinevere." There. She'd said it right out loud. The worst was over. But even as Phoebe tried to reassure herself of this, an invisible hand seemed to be clutching at her very being, deep inside, twisting her pounding heart and constricting her breathing.

One of the things that Phoebe liked best about Annie was how very accepting she was. Phoebe could just as easily have told her that she planned to jump over the moon atop the fabled cow, and still Annie would have given her that familiar, silent blessing.

Once Phoebe's breathing had returned to normal, the two huddled down into the sheets, which had been carefully turned back at the top to insulate against the scratchy pink wool blanket that Granny had given her and waited for a peaceful sleep to overtake them.

Sleep didn't come easily that night, and when it did, it could hardly be called peaceful. Phoebe must have faced the dreaded Camelot auditions a dozen times throughout the night. She heard her name called and walked to centre stage naked! She was called again and walked to centre stage on crutches, then bald, and one time she appeared to be 100 years old!

By the time that morning finally arrived, Phoebe Buttanshaw was in crisis. She wanted to run far away, but she didn't. As always Phoebe tried to do the responsible thing. She jumped up two minutes before the alarm was set to shake the sleep from her, and she dashed directly towards the wardrobe without so much as a glance into the clown mirror.

Phoebe tried on every combination of outfits that day hoping to find something that looked slightly royal. Her mind was a blank. She couldn't picture Guinevere at all, let alone convert herself into a 13 year-old facsimile. Eventually, Phoebe decided to attend the audition in her school uniform. After all, everyone would be arriving at the try-outs directly from classes, and she didn't want to be the only one who carried a change of clothes around all day. No, she would keep a low profile until the very last moment when she would simply allow her previously hidden talent to bowl them all over. It would be such a moment of triumph for her. Suddenly Phoebe found herself calming down just enough to manage to put one foot in front of the other in the general direction of Fielder's School.

As she walked, Phoebe thought of all the great actors and actresses who, over the years, had confessed to being very shy people in their personal lives. Yet, somehow, when they walked onto the stage they would magically be transformed into the character of the moment.

That's it! That is what would happen to Phoebe that very day at the female auditions for the Fielder's School production of Camelot. Little by little her optimism grew and the school slowly came into view.

Phoebe had 15 minutes to spare before her Latin class so she picked up the latest edition of the school magazine. 'Kip O'Conner to Play King Arthur' screeched the headline. Phoebe felt her nerves return as she quickly scanned the words.

'Kip is a new addition to Fielder's School, but at his former school he not only starred in many productions but also lent his hand to writing, directing, and choreographing.' Choreographing? Phoebe's glowing admiration was only momentarily dampened as she remembered Kip's words in Ripple

Park that Saturday evening. "Besides I can't dance…."

There wasn't time to dwell on questionable choreography credits. Latin class beckoned, and so Phoebe answered its call.

Mrs Lafayette was a peculiar teacher. Fielder's School seemed to attract peculiar teachers in general, but Mrs Lafayette was a peculiar teacher in particular. Phoebe had always thought of her as being as ancient as the subject she taught; but she supposed that, in reality, she must only be about the age of her very own parents, which, although old by some standards, wasn't nearly as old as Mrs Lafayette's hair or shoes would suggest.

On that morning Mrs Lafayette stood before her pupils wearing a very sensible brown suit with even more sensible brown lace-up orthopaedic brogues on her thick feet. Phoebe had noticed that Mrs Lafayette owned the exact same style of shoe in brown for Autumn, black for Winter, and white for Summer. Practical, Phoebe thought, very practical. Then Phoebe made a mental promise to herself to never wear a brown suit.

The story emerging from the pages of the Latin workbook about little twin brothers raised by wolves could not hold Phoebe's attention any more than Mrs Lafayette's sniffling nose and watery eyes. Only in passing did Phoebe wonder whether the hunched, grey lady might be crying or whether it was merely an allergy attack. Mrs Lafayette held a reputation at Fielder's School for being an easy target, and more cruel boys at the school seemed to see an irresistible challenge to bringing the old woman to tears.

Although she was normally a very concerned student, Phoebe couldn't help but be preoccupied with her own problems throughout that morning.

At long last the ringing of the bell told Phoebe that she could leave the Latin class behind. As the students filed through the oaken door, Mrs Lafayette's quivering voice asked two of the boys who'd been seated at the back of the small classroom to remain behind for a talk.

"Oh dear, they're at it again," Phoebe thought. But her concerns soon abandoned Mrs Lafayette and the naughty boys.

It was lunchtime at Fielder's School. Would this October Friday never end? The school food held no appeal for Phoebe, and she would gladly have skipped lunch altogether except that noontime break was the perfect opportunity to catch up on gossip; and gossip that day meant Camelot auditions. It was on everyone's lips. Who would be Guinevere? All the drama society regulars would naturally, be trying for the coveted part. Would it be Jeanine Robertson or Sasha Kennick or, Phoebe's worried eyes darted from pretty face to pretty face, or Cricket Allison? Oh no, not this time.

Phoebe was certain that the gods would smile down on her just this once. After all, it was the law of averages, wasn't it? She would have to triumph eventually, wouldn't she?

Phoebe held fiercely onto what little confidence remained inside her while all around the voices of chattering teenage Guinevere's tried to chip away at her dream.

And so the afternoon passed in a blur of dreaded anticipation. At 4:30 it was time to gather in the auditorium amongst the other hopefuls.

"At least it's just the girls," Phoebe whispered under her breath, trying to convince herself that it could have been worse when suddenly it became obviously, blatantly, dreadfully worse.

Seated in the middle of the stage, which was empty except for a large plastic tree stump from the Fielder's prop department, was Kip O'Conner. Kip always seemed to be perched on top of trees or hiding inside of trees, so perhaps Phoebe shouldn't have been quite so shocked by his presence on the Fielder's prop dept's plastic tree. But she was. After all, this was the day of auditions for the female cast.

Phoebe's mind was racing nearly as fast as her heart. What shall I do? Shall I stay? Shall I go? Nimbly, Kip hopped from the tree onto the bare wooden floor producing the only sound in the hushed room. Phoebe thought that he really was quite elfin, compact in a nice sort of way, but just a bit taller than Phoebe, which pleased her. He walked right to the edge of the stage until his toes hung precariously over the orchestra pit.

"Hello. I'm Kip O'Conner, and I'll be reading with each of you today, so relax and enjoy. Let's get started!"

With that, Mr Howlett, the drama teacher, picked up his clipboard and called out the first name. Poor Penelope Phipp was the victim. Phoebe felt pure sympathy for the quiet girl with the long plaits as she picked up the Camelot script and approached Kip on the tree. It wouldn't be easy to pass as Guinevere while wearing a Fielder's blazer and thick grey socks. Still, Phoebe felt that Penelope gave it a good try although it was obvious that her voice couldn't quite conceal the nerves that she was experiencing along with every other girl in the room.

One by one the hopeful candidates read from the increasingly ragged pages. The scenes were chosen by Mr Howlett so there was no chance of guessing the mood or pace of what was to be expected from each reading. Phoebe was wondering what he would select for her when she heard him call out the next name, "Cricket Allison."

Phoebe suddenly sat very straight in her chair and leaned back as far as she could without sliding onto the floor. Her eyes were straining to see from which side Cricket would enter. When she finally emerged Phoebe couldn't believe it!

Cricket was the only girl there who had discarded the confines of the school uniform in exchange for the most beautiful long tapestry skirt that Phoebe had ever laid eyes upon! The skirt flowed onto the stage with a mature sort of grace that caught Phoebe off guard. As she looked at the petite frame and the pixie-like face framed by yards of white ruffles, Phoebe felt a familiar resignation sweep through her suddenly limp body.

"Cricket Allison will be Kip's Guinevere," Phoebe wasn't sure if she shouted the words out loud or whether they just bounced around inside her head so violently that it felt like a scream. Phoebe tried to regain her composure thinking, Cricket always gets what she wants, or rather Cricket always gets what I want! Phoebe's thoughts were so loudly overpowering that she didn't seem to hear the lines being spoken by Kip or Cricket. It was all a bad dream, and then it was over; and Mr Howlett was again at centre stage with his clipboard.

"Phoebe Buttanshaw, please."

Phoebe stood for a second and then ran to the door leading into the backstage area. She took a panicked look around her. She was in a green room with a few simple chairs at one side. The other side of the room was reserved for a long dancers' bar where so many Fielder's students had warmed up before dashing on stage. The entire length of the wall was mirrored so Phoebe couldn't avoid the all too glaring image reflected back at her.

There stood a tall, gangly girl in a grey blazer and knee socks. More obvious than that, though, was the gigantic pair of round glasses jumping from her face. In Phoebe's hysterical state she could see nothing in the mirror other than the distorted lenses.

As she stood frozen in front of the mirror, she caught sight of the reflection of a small, pretty girl exiting stage left, a petite girl with a stylish haircut, ruffled blouse, and, most of all, not wearing glasses. Phoebe pulled off the offending spectacles and stumbled up the three steps that led to the stage. At least now she felt she had a chance.

Mr Howlett placed the Camelot script into the trembling, outstretched hands. Without her glasses, Phoebe couldn't be certain, but she thought she saw a reassuring nod from Kip O'Conner. When Phoebe failed to move, Mr Howlett gently guided her to the plastic tree upon which sat a 14 year-old boy with curly locks and, thank goodness, wearing a school blazer. Both their scripts were turned to page 48, and Phoebe could see that a glaring yellow marking pen had mapped out her lines.

Kip stared down from the tree and looked into Phoebe's red face. "You are like a morning in May," he managed to say with some conviction.

What? Was he talking to her, Phoebe wondered. Her eyes shot over the script, which was now turning soggy from all the sweaty hands that had clutched it throughout the long afternoon. In her dreams, Phoebe had auditioned naked, on crutches, and riddled with age, but she had never auditioned blind until that moment. Without her beloved and most hated spectacles, Phoebe could not make out a single word.

"Go on, Phoebe," Mr Howlett's patient voice gave her encouragement but it was all useless.

Phoebe was only happy that she couldn't see Kip's expression as she dropped page 48 of the Camelot script and flew back into the green room. Grabbing the discarded glasses, Phoebe fled the auditorium and Fielder's School. There was no chance of holding back the floods of tears so Phoebe didn't even try. She turned toward her home and put all her concentration on walking. The stares from passersby didn't faze her. Nothing mattered at that moment except finding refuge in the safety of her own little bedroom.

Once inside the Buttanshaw house, Phoebe seemed to float up the stairs. In what felt like one smooth movement, she threw her glasses onto the chest of drawers, grabbed Annie from her shelf, and dived under the pink blanket. Phoebe didn't join her family for dinner that evening. She just held her old friend very tightly to her chest and waited for morning.

Wart, a Rabbit

It was Saturday morning, and Phoebe Buttanshaw was in a box. Of course, she wasn't literally in a box, but she did feel quite isolated from everything around her. She was oblivious to the normal Saturday morning routines which carried on throughout the house as she reviewed over and over in her mind the catastrophe of the Camelot audition.

Phoebe was truly miserable and was bathing in that misery until Mrs Buttanshaw knocked on her bedroom door. That sight that greeted her when she pushed back the door was one of maximum unhappiness, the kind felt most harshly by the hearts of sensitive 13 year-old girls. There was Phoebe, still firmly embracing the always patient Annie, and still wearing her white school blouse from the previous day. Phoebe peered with some trepidation over the pink wool blanket which was pulled right up to her nose.

Mrs Buttanshaw had seen the symptoms of gloom before and hoped her words might offer some relief. "Come on, Button," Mrs Buttanshaw always called her daughter Button at such times. "There's someone here to see you."

The words didn't give the immediate reaction that had been hoped for, and Mrs Buttanshaw found herself coaxing Phoebe from her bed and having to use even more persuasion to get her into her usual Saturday clothes consisting of jeans and sweater. Phoebe was reaching for the door when Mrs Buttanshaw asked, "Don't you want your glasses, Button?"

Phoebe's face screwed into an expression that was dismayed and confused. "Want them? Do I want my glasses?" Phoebe thought about it for a few seconds. Well, in hindsight she wished that she'd had them at the audition yesterday, but, on a larger scale, it was really impossible for Phoebe to admit that she genuinely wanted them. Still, deciding that the casual question from her mother didn't really warrant a grand analysis into the issue of whether or not Phoebe, in fact, felt desire for her glasses, the slumped girl held out her hand, and the spectacles in question were instantly in her grasp. At least she'd be able to actually see the staircase now, she decided, and moved hesitantly towards the downstairs hall.

So, who wanted to see Phoebe on this Saturday morning anyway? She had pretty much decided that no one would ever want to see her again, but to have a visitor so soon after the occurrences of the previous day was shockingly unexpected.

When Phoebe caught sight of the person awaiting her, she still didn't know who it was. There, in front of her, stood a most peculiar looking child. She was pretty sure it was a boy, but his hair was very nearly to his shoulders and cut in a shaggy, unisex style. He must have been around 10 years old although it was difficult to say. He had a high forehead and freckles scattered across a broad nose. He was much shorter than Phoebe, naturally, but with a rounded tummy and substantial shoulders. A sturdy little figure, all in all, she thought, as she looked the boy over. Then the child smiled and took on a different appearance altogether. Phoebe thought that he had a nice smile, and there was something decidedly familiar about the way his cheeks dimpled.

"I've brought something for you," the boy spoke for the first time. "Here."

Chubby little hands held out a box with holes punched into it. Phoebe's curiosity was beginning to get the better of her so she reached out, accepting the offering. The boy's mission was complete, and he turned to go. When he reached the door he looked back at Phoebe and the box.

"Oh, I'm Oliver O'Conner. Well, Ollie really. There's a note inside from Kip. See you." And, with that, the little urchin ran off into the Saturday morning.

Phoebe didn't waste any time in opening the box. She couldn't believe her eyes when she came face to face with the most beautiful angora bunny she could ever have imagined. He was fawn coloured with huge brown eyes and the longest down-turned ears that Phoebe had ever seen on a rabbit.

Next to the little animal Phoebe found the folded paper with Kip's message on it. A small shudder went down her back as she opened the note. It read: 'Please take good care of this creature whose name is Wart. Augie and I will be at the fallen tree in Ripple Park at 2:00. See you there.'

The spirit inside of Phoebe that had been so low just moments before was instantly soaring somewhere miles above her! This roller coaster effect took even Phoebe by surprise. What could it mean? Phoebe was suddenly just so very, very happy. She had her very own lop-eared rabbit, and she was seeing Kip in Ripple Park. The day was certainly turning out far better than she'd ever expected.

Mrs Buttanshaw had a most pleased smile on her face when Phoebe danced into the roomy kitchen with her furry little companion. This kitchen had been the centre of the family home all of Phoebe's life. While many families tended to gather in the living room, the Buttanshaws seemed to be forever settled at the big kitchen table. It was there that problems got solved, important announcements got made, and joys were shared.

Mr Buttanshaw was still at the table enjoying the leisure of a Saturday morning cup of coffee when Phoebe decided to share her joyous news of the new bunny along with the problem of where he would reside.

"His name is Wart," Phoebe was talking faster than she'd ever talked before. "And he needs a place to live."

Both of Phoebe's parents initially agreed that Wart was a very ugly name for such a pretty creature, but Phoebe explained that Wart had been Merlin's pet name for King Arthur when he was just a boy. Her enthusiasm for the name and for the story attached to it soon convinced Mr and Mrs Buttanshaw that perhaps Wart wasn't such a bad name after all.

Within minutes Phoebe had urged her father out of his chair and into the garden where preparations began for the building of a hutch. It couldn't be a ho-hum hutch. Phoebe was adamant that it should be a hutch fit for a king. Mr Buttanshaw promised Phoebe and Wart that the result would be a castle of a hutch, and he set about the task at hand. Phoebe helped with whatever she could until she realised that the morning had slipped away, and she would have to get herself to Ripple Park at once.

As she walked towards the park, Phoebe thought that it must surely be the most beautiful day she'd ever seen. It was cool with a brisk breeze, but the sun was showering everything with its yellow rays, or it could be that Phoebe was suddenly seeing everything in a golden light. Phoebe loved October, and she loved Ripple Park. She felt like she had wings on her ankles as they carried her toward the old fallen tree in the centre of the park.

Before Phoebe could see those who awaited her arrival, she heard the excited bark of her little friend, Augie. He seemed to be encouraging her to hurry, and so she did. She rushed so fast that she didn't even have time to rethink the horror of the day before. It was dear Augie who first caught Phoebe's eye. He was in his playful position with his front half lying down but his back half held high with the little tail pointing straight up. Then, from out of the taller grass emerged another shaggy dog. Augie had brought a friend! She was silver, had longer hair than Augie, and was slightly larger. They had obviously played together before and seemed to be taking delight in the sharing of secret games.

"In Camelot it never rains till after sunset…" Phoebe heard the words coming from behind the tree.

Without thought or inhibition she answered, "By 6:00 AM the clouds all disappear."

Out popped Kip O'Conner with eyes twinkling, and the two voices united to say, "In all the world there's simply not a more congenial spot for happy-ever-aftering than here in Camelot."

Phoebe found herself laughing for the first time in a very long time. Kip laughed right along with her, and when the two of them looked at Augie and Shu-Shu, his dishevelled friend, they were sure that the dogs were joining them in the private joke.

That afternoon in Ripple Park was glorious for Phoebe. She was, at least for a day, Kip O'Conner's Guinevere. Together they fought off the evil Black Knight, and they marvelled at Merlin's magical forest where one could merge with nature and speak with rabbits or dance with joyous young dogs in a way that can only be experienced by those who haven't yet discarded the innocence of childhood.

At last Phoebe had found herself a friend; a living, breathing, laughing friend in whom she felt enough trust to embody her with the strength to destroy "the thing" and to cast off unwarranted inhibitions and to wear her glasses and to be herself.

On Monday morning the Camelot casting notice was posted as dozens of fresh, young faces searched for their names. Leading the list was the name of the Fielder's High School girl who would play the coveted part of Guinevere. Phoebe tried to act nonchalant as she paused and made a sideways glance at the notice board.

What was this? Did her eyes deceive her? The role of Lady Guinevere would go to Penelope Phipp! Phoebe felt a small gasp escape from her mouth. Impossible, she thought.

Before Phoebe had time to digest the announcement, the small person of Cricket Allison plunged through the crowd. Phoebe couldn't help herself; she just had to observe Cricket's reaction. Whether this need came from curiosity or relief or 13 year-old cruelty was a mystery even to Phoebe. Prepared to feel elation, however, she found that quite the opposite feeling overtook her as she watched Cricket Allison's perfectly made-up eyes brim with tears, and then she was gone. She ran toward the girls' bathrooms looking much smaller than ever.

Perhaps Phoebe and Cricket actually had something in common after all. For one short-lived minute in the long hallways at Fielder's School Phoebe felt genuine compassion for her longstanding rival. Together, and separately, they had longed for and lost the chance to share the magic of Camelot at the side of Kip O'Conner.

Six weeks later Camelot played to a packed audience in the Fielder's School auditorium. Phoebe sat enthralled by the story and by the romance and by Kip. Her emotions were touched on every level, and she wept at the end along with many others. Penelope Phipp was a perfect Guinevere with her beautiful waistlength plaits and a sweet singing voice.

In the end, everything worked out just as it should. It was the first of December, and all was right with the world.

Angels

Phoebe Buttanshaw was a dreamer who sang Christmas carols all year round. It was only natural then that December should be her favourite month and that Christmas should be her favourite holiday. She loved everything about it – the frosty air biting at her ears and nose, the smell of evergreen wreaths and trees, the lights, the sounds, the smiles, the secrets, but most of all Phoebe loved the angels. She always drew angels on her Christmas cards, kept an angel high at the top of her Christmas tree, and often appeared in her dreams sporting a full set of white, feathery angel wings. Phoebe had heard others relate their own stories of dreams where they could fly through the skies, and she always wondered whether they, too, wore the wings of snow-white angels while they slept. So far, she hadn't heard of anyone else who shared her secret longing. Oh, anyone who spoke of a dream that possessed one with the sudden freedom of flight did so with certain enthusiasm; but for Phoebe there was quite a separate attraction. To proudly wear the white wings was her dream. The act of flying the skies of her dreams came second.

As she emerged from a disappointedly dreamless sleep that cold early December morning, Phoebe felt a chill travel up her body as her feet reluctantly touched the wooden floor next to her bed. The cold made her move with unusual speed as she dashed for her warmest sweater, ignoring the clowns in the mirror and even ignoring her old friend Annie. After layering on as much clothing as would squeeze under her school blazer, Phoebe quit shivering enough to face the day.

Each morning began for Phoebe with a visit to the beautiful Wart. He was particularly happy to see her on this cold morning, for she always brought all of his favourite things – fresh food, water, and lots of thick warm straw for keeping the December cold at bay. Phoebe and Wart had indeed grown to be great friends since he'd come to live with the Buttanshaws. He trusted Phoebe completely; and she trusted Wart completely too, often sneaking him into her bedroom for a secret late night visit which was something completely against the house rules.

With chores behind her and breakfast out of the way, Phoebe began the familiar journey towards Fielder's School. She felt that she knew every crack in the pavement and every brick in the wall intimately, for she often spoke to them by name as she passed by.

Having time to spare following her increased morning speed, Phoebe decided to walk past Kip's house for a change. The fresh, cool air put a spring in Phoebe's step, and it was not time at all before she found herself nearing the fence that enclosed the O'Conner garden.

Under the garden gate was the wonderful, black nose of her little buddy, Augie, who remained on constant vigil either at the front door or the back gate. He felt it was his duty to keep watch and inform the family of any visitors. Knowing Phoebe as well as he did, Augie offered only a friendly greeting when she opened the gate and moved towards the house.

The garden had taken on a rather stark appearance in its winter months. The frost had chased back much of the overgrowth making the overall impression one of immense space. As Phoebe observed the changing face of the O'Conner garden, Kip suddenly bolted from the door hot on Augie's heels. Augie possessed the greater speed and agility at such an early hour, and he dashed into a thick hedge just out of Kip's grasp.

"Augie! Give me back my toast!" Kip shouted into the silent hedge, giving Phoebe reason to smile. Kip turned to see Phoebe halfway up the garden path. "He does it every morning," Kip said by way of explanation.

Without further words, Phoebe and Kip opened the gate and began the walk towards school. Suddenly, Phoebe felt that her legs had been knocked from under her. She'd been hit by a speeding ball of silver fur as she turned the corner. It was Augie's funny friend, Shu-Shu, who was obviously in a mad rush to some unspoken destination.

Phoebe had already spoken the words, "Excuse me," before she realised that it was one of the neighbourhood dogs that she was speaking to. Shu-Shu didn't slow her pace and seemed uninterested in apologies as she continued on her way.

Kip and Phoebe walked and laughed, talking of dogs and Christmas. They stopped briefly to peer into the window of Phoebe's favourite shop called 'Over the Moon'. She had kept a close watch on that shop window twice a day every school day for many years now and knew at a glance when it had been altered, and altered it certainly had been. Sometime between the previous afternoon and that early morning, Christmas had come to Over the Moon. Snowflakes clung to the corners of all the small window frames and golden stars hung from above, shimmering in the glow of tiny fairy lights; but, best of all, a lovely white angel looked down at the scene with approval.

Phoebe's eyes opened wide at the sight of the angelic wings. She looked at Kip's face and saw reflected in his eyes the same sense of joy and appreciation. Somehow, the two rarely needed words to communicate. It was a long time before either of them moved from the spot in front of the shop window; but, eventually, school beckoned so they made their way to the Fielder's doors, parting reluctantly to begin their day.

Each of the classes at Fielder's School from both the primary school and the high school were in the midst of preparations for their contribution to the annual Christmas pageant. There would be choral offering galore and a few readings on offer. The drama society had promised that they would assist in something special as a finale. Phoebe loved the Christmas pageant dearly for it was always over-flowing with her favourite music and sentiments.

That afternoon the auditorium was packed to capacity with Fielder students of all ages and sizes.

There was a feeling of merry disorganisation as various groups trod onto the stage, joined together in song, and made hasty exits. Phoebe's group sang, 'It Came Upon a Midnight Clear', one of her favourites.

Perhaps it was the safety in numbers or maybe the season, but Phoebe didn't feel the slightest bit anxious as her voice joined the others in song.

Following the musical phase of that first rehearsal, Kip took centre stage to announce that the drama society would be auditioning for participants for the big finale to the Christmas pageant. He would need shepherds and wise men and angels.

Angels? Phoebe's heart skipped a beat, but she soon regained a sense of perspective. Recalling her last attempt at auditioning for a dramatic role in that very auditorium, Phoebe decided immediately that she would not be joining the try-outs again. After all, she felt quite pleased with herself to be singing along to 'It Came Upon a Midnight Clear'.

Phoebe allowed the day of the drama society's auditions to come and to go without her attendance. She'd barely seen Kip who had been working madly on arrangements for his contribution to the Christmas presentation.

It was with great dismay, then, when three days later Phoebe caught a glimpse of her name jumping from the school notice board. Was there another Phoebe at Fielder's School? Could there be two Phoebe Buttanshaws? That didn't really seem a likely explanation. Phoebe stood in front of the notice board and squinted. She put her face so close to the board that she felt the rough surface hit the end of her freckled nose. She looked at the name sideways and out of the corner of each eye. The angle couldn't alter what she saw. There just could be no logical explanation for it, but there it was as plain as the nose on Phoebe's bewildered face. The drama society's cast announcement clearly stated that the lead angel in the host of heavenly angels would be played in this year's Christmas pageant by one Phoebe Buttanshaw!

"Congratulations. You're an angel."

Phoebe was so deep in her own thoughts that she jumped slightly at the unexpected interruption. She turned to find Kip O'Conner looking very pleased with himself.

"I……..don't fly. I mean, I can't act. I mean, I didn't audition…." Phoebe was unable to find the right words or ask the many questions colliding madly in her brain.

"Doesn't matter. It's all settled." Kip seemed his usual, confident self; but Phoebe was still trying to work it all out in her exhausted mind when she saw the tiny print at the bottom of the announcement. 'Presented by Fielder's Drama Society. Direction and casting by Kip O'Conner.'

As Kip turned to walk to his next class, he shouted over his shoulder, "Merry Christmas! See you at rehearsal!" And then he was away, prancing down the long hallway with curls bouncing along with each step.

Phoebe didn't think, couldn't think, any further about what had just happened. She was in a state of complete confusion. Her classes seemed to be only dreams throughout the long afternoon, and she was merely a sleepwalking observer.

When finally the school day came to a finish she walked, trancelike, into the auditorium where Kip was busy arranging tiny angels and not so tiny shepherds as if the players were pieces in a lifesize chess set. Phoebe was awed by his ability to control the crowd of youngsters. It was obvious that he was enjoying the exercise and that the enjoyment was returned by those involved.

Phoebe walked to the stage and allowed herself to become part of the aura of excitement. She was soon delegated to the back part of stage left where she was surrounded by her host of supporting angels. They didn't look much like angels, Phoebe thought as her eyes looked over each child in turn.

There was that strange boy from Phoebe's Latin class, Kenny Hargreaves. All she really knew about Kenny was that he was afraid of dirt and spent most of his time avoiding it or trying to wash it away. Causing mild chaos amongst the angel crew was Ollie O'Conner. He was in his element on the stage and kept bursting into song and dance routines in numerous outrageous styles. Keeping Ollie in tow would require some doing, Phoebe decided. Next to Ollie stood Ellen Nordwell, a quiet girl from the primary school who always seemed to have a nasty head cold and occasionally sucked her thumb. Why Kip had selected this unlikely group to play the heavenly host was a mystery to Phoebe as her eyes danced from one fact to the next until, out of the blue, appeared a young girl of about 10 years of age who most surely was an angel. She had long, dark hair which fell in a mess of waves, framing a face most certainly made of china.

The girl walked towards Phoebe and asked if she was in the correct place to be an angel. Phoebe assured her that she most definitely was. The child introduced herself.

"I'm Jeanette Winkworth, but I'm always called Winkie. I'm really an artist, but I thought it might be fun to be an angel for a while."

The little girl's wide, blue eyes came alive with the prospect. Phoebe couldn't fault Kip's choice of Winkie to be a Christmas angel. She was without flaw amongst the sea of imperfect youth that surrounded her.

That first meeting consisted mainly of formulating small groups and handing out information regarding rehearsal dates, costume requirements, and general logistics for where the many players would be placed. With only two weeks to arrange the scene, there was much to be done by everyone.

Those two weeks raced by in a haze of shepherds' robes and heavenly carols until it was at last the evening of the Fielder's Christmas pageant.

Standing in the green room in the wings off the stage, Phoebe felt a strange mixture of excitement and terror. She'd never known quite such contradicting forces to be at work inside her.

The pageant was progressing in the usual way with songs flowing from the youngest first and gradually working up to the older students. The auditorium was full of proud parents and prouder grandparents.

Finally, Cricket Allison strolled gracefully to the microphone to give a reading about the meaning of Christmas. Phoebe felt no jealousy in this holy season. Besides, because Cricket's reading came immediately before the big finale, it meant that Cricket was unable to participate which pleased Phoebe greatly. All that Cricket's solo performance meant to Phoebe on this occasion was that it was time to get into costume. She glanced into the mirrors that surrounded her and tried to make her hair appear more angelic. There was no question of removing her glasses after what had happened last time.

Mrs Howlett, the wife of the drama coach, was busy backstage pushing small angels into white choir robes and fixing halos made of tinsel onto bobbing heads. The wings had been made by fixing kitchen foil onto cardboard cut-outs. Somehow, it all seemed to work, and the Fielder's students looked suitably, and surprisingly, angelic.

Mrs Howlett spied Phoebe who looked rather lost in the crowded room. She waved her to come nearer; and when approached, she was met by a sight such as she'd never seen before. It was the most heavenly, perfect pair of white wings that Phoebe could have ever dreamt. In dress rehearsal Phoebe had worn her white robes, but the wings had been considered too fragile to use until the actual performance. She had assumed that she would have kitchen foil wings like the others, but that certainly was not the case.

Mrs Howlett sensed the awe in Phoebe's approach, and so it was with great enjoyment that she helped her into her long wished for angel wings. Standing transfixed in front of the full length mirrors, Phoebe felt so full of Christmas joy that she was sure that she would be able to fly on her own that night rather than rely on the complex rigging and wires. Just over her shoulder, reflected in the glass, Phoebe could see the slim figure of Kip O'Conner. There was a knowing smile planted firmly on his face, and then he said, "Let's go!"

The time had come to put all the hard work into action, and Kip really had his chance to shine. Phoebe was amazed, but it all went like clockwork. The shepherds were in the field, the wise men appeared as wise as 12 year-old boys know how, and the angels were in their places.

It was at precisely that moment that Phoebe, with white wings spread wide, floated down from the heavens above Fielder's School auditorium to announce in her bravest voice that all should rejoice. As she made her declaration, Mrs Buttanshaw succumbed to the fate of generations of mothers of school age children before her. Tears flowed freely down her cheeks, as she was overwhelmed with a mother's love.

It was truly Phoebe's dream come true, and it was over much too quickly. Phoebe left the stage riding high on a cloud of emotion. Following such a once in a lifetime experience came the disappointing chore of changing back into a 13 year-old girl's jeans, and Phoebe just barely managed it.

The pageant also marked the dismissal of school for the long Christmas break, which only served to enhance the mighty excitement bouncing off the keyed up mass of high-spirited performers.

Parents formed an anxious reception line where they received their children as the stage was left behind. Arms were flying in all directions as embraces were handed out generously. Phoebe graciously accepted her share of hugs but declined the offer of a ride home. She was far too elated and wished to walk beneath the heavens forever, or at least for the 10 minutes that her walk home would require.

Bundled up in scarf and heavy coat and warmest boots, Phoebe began her journey. How could she have known that emotions ride a roller coaster all of their own, and what feels like the top of the world can quickly be dashed to the depths.

Phoebe turned the first corner in the route she'd walked a thousand times before, but something was terribly different. There by the edge of the road was a small figure hovering over a bundle of silver fur. Who? What? Phoebe looked over her shoulder for someone to help, but only darkness followed her. She ran to the street and froze in her footsteps, unable to move or speak.

It was an animal and next to it was a tiny angel with long, dark hair. Winkie was still wearing her halo of gold tinsel, and she had strapped her foil wings on top of her little red duffle coat. Phoebe had never experienced grief before, but she felt it at that moment.

The dog's front paw was outstretched, and the angel stroked it tenderly. "It's my dog. It's Shu-Shu," the voice was barely audible through the quivering lips.

Still Phoebe was frozen. Suddenly, out of nowhere, help appeared. Someone was gently wrapping Shu-Shu in a grey blanket. Then his arm embraced the poor, broken angel. Phoebe moved a step closer. It was Kip O'Conner.

It seemed like an eternity before Winkie's father appeared in the family car and whisked his precious daughter and her equally precious little dog into the night.

After the car had left, Phoebe and Kip sat on the kerb in silence for a very long time. The sky had never seemed quite so black or the stars quite so bright. Kip's eyes were riveted to the street as

Phoebe examined his face over and over. It was the face of kindness and generosity of spirit.

An angel…. Phoebe thought, without wings or halo, but certainly an angel without a shred of doubt.

And Phoebe Buttanshaw had always loved angels.

The Science Fair

It was as if she'd been trapped in a slow motion Hollywood horror movie. Phoebe Buttanshaw heard Mr Carmichael's instructions, but her brain rebelled at the command.

"Phoebe. Pay attention. I'll only repeat it one more time." Mr Carmichael was using his most stern voice, and Phoebe felt her hot face tingle as the eyes of all the science students stared in her direction.

"Your lab partner for this term will be Cricket Allison, and your first project will be due in two weeks' time."

Phoebe tried to reply but decided that a nod would suffice. Mr Carmichael seemed to accept it as an acknowledgement and moved his attention on to the rest of the class. Cricket Allison, in the meantime, had collected books and pencils in her small hands and relocated herself at Phoebe's lab table.

"Why is your face so red?" Cricket asked just loudly enough to be heard by most of the budding scientists in the room.

Phoebe gritted her teeth and stared at her notebook, knowing only too well that such a comment was guaranteed to turn her from hot pink to beet red in an instant.

Luckily, Phoebe didn't have time to justify her complexion to Cricket because Mr Carmichael suddenly demanded everyone's strict attention. He was a short, squat man with thinning crew cut hair and a bump on one side of his nose, and he seemed to be forever irritated. Phoebe didn't really like Mr Carmichael any more than she liked science. Science can hold no attraction for a dreamer. When Phoebe Buttanshaw's eyes turned to the clouds above, her thoughts were only with the animal shapes they formed or the angels they might shelter. She had no interest in whether the cloud which danced in the face of the sun happened to be the cumulus nimbus variety or not. Hence, the hour spent in the company of Mr Carmichael, Cricket Allison, and an abundance of test tubes was not one which Phoebe anticipated with much enthusiasm even under the best of circumstances; but the thought of any kind of partnership with Cricket magnified Phoebe's apprehension to the maximum.

When the science class finally came to an end, Phoebe leapt to her feet, grabbed her belongings, and dashed toward the door leaving Cricket on her own. Perhaps, she thought, if she just ignored the situation it would sort itself out. Of course, that solution belonged to Phoebe Buttanshaw, the dreamer. The reality usually proved to demand a more active approach, and that was Phoebe's downfall.

Avoiding Cricket Allison had never been difficult for Phoebe. Why, they had lived on the same street all their lives and Phoebe usually managed it skilfully. Interacting with the Elm Road pixie was quite a different story, however.

When Phoebe and Cricket were 6 years old, their well-meaning mothers decided that they should become firm friends. Phoebe never understood how or why this came about, and at age 6 she wasn't included in decisions such as who would become her best friend. And so one Saturday morning over seven years ago, Cricket Allison was delivered to the Buttanshaw home and presented to Phoebe.

Phoebe could still picture Mrs Buttanshaw's face, all aglow, as she waited and watched the two little girls. It was as if, in her mind, she'd just given Phoebe a magnificent gift for which the 6 year-old would be eternally grateful. Phoebe's reaction didn't exactly live up to her mother's expectations. She merely looked at the small person and then turned toward her bedroom where she retreated to the sanctuary shared by her true friend, Annie.

It wasn't long before Cricket found her way into Phoebe's precious bedroom and made herself at home, much to the disbelief of poor Phoebe.

Cricket looked curiously at Phoebe and then at Annie.

"Where are your good dolls?" she asked.

"Annie is my good doll and my only doll," Phoebe snapped at the impertinence of such a question. She saw under Cricket's arm a perfectly turned out ceramic-faced doll with hundreds of blonde ringlets on her perfectly shaped head with ruffles enveloping every inch of her perfectly shaped body. Phoebe had always refused to allow such creatures to share her world. She considered them creepy and unpleasant in much the same way that she felt about Cricket Allison.

""Okay, then," Cricket had decided to keep the conversation rolling. "Let's play hospital and your dolly is hurt."

That was the point of no return for Phoebe as Cricket's stubby, manicured fingers pried Annie from her clasp. Within seconds Cricket had managed to twist poor Annie's arm round and round until it separated completely from her body!

Beyond that Phoebe's memory was blurred by years of unspoken contempt and rivalry. All tat Phoebe knew for certain was that there was no way for her to participate calmly in any partnership with Cricket Allison. No way at all.

It was deep in such thoughts that Phoebe walked home from school that afternoon. "It just can't be done," she thought over and over to herself.

"What can't be done?" Phoebe turned to find Kip O'Conner by her side, reading her thoughts as usual.

"Oh, lots of things," Phoebe said avoiding the true problem. "Can't walk across the Pacific Ocean or sit on top of a cloud without falling through it..... just lots of things."

And so the conversation went until Kip and Phoebe stopped to examine the new Over the Moon window display. Although Phoebe preferred the Christmas display to all others, she was most intrigued to find carved wooden gnomes and wood sprites of every description peering back at her through the glass panes. Each one had a unique and often comical facial expression. As the two friends debated the qualities of each small figure they were oblivious to the excited shopper exiting Over the Moon.

"Oh, Phoebe! Kip! Look what I've just bought! It's a present for Mummy!" squealed a manic Cricket Allison.

Phoebe stood speechless, wondering how this person could dare to invade such a private moment. Kip, however, was his usual charming self and expressed interest in Cricket's purchase. With minimal encouragement, out of the bag popped the laciest, ruffliest pillow that Phoebe had ever seen.

"Read it! Read it!" Cricket demanded.

So the two poked at the pink embroidered letters with some dismay. The words were 'Always My Mother – Now My Friend.' Phoebe felt that she might be sick but managed to control the urge.

"Oh, very touching," Kip remained true to form which brought a pleased smile to Cricket's face as well as a wry grin to Kip's.

"Well, we have to go," Phoebe interjected.

"Good," Cricket didn't seem to get the message as she added, "I'll walk with you."

The walk home, which had begun so pleasantly, suddenly seemed shrouded by a dark cloud. Phoebe sulked as Cricket and Kip talked and laughed. To distract herself from the situation, Phoebe decided to direct her energy toward something more constructive and so tried to visualise Cricket Allison living on a sheep farm in Australia. She'd read somewhere an article about 'positive visualisation', which had insisted that one could alter one's condition simply by imagining that it was different.

Certainly worth a try, Phoebe had decided; and so it was with great disappointment that she completed her mental exercise only to find Cricket Allison still firmly planted between herself and Kip.

Even worse than that, she saw something that she hadn't noticed before. It wasn't anything that she could name. It was more of an intangible thing – a feeling that seemed to be bouncing off of her two companions. A shiver made its way down Phoebe's back. She felt hot and cold at the same time when she saw Kip make direct eye contact with Cricket, remaining just a second too long. Phoebe's mouth went completely dry as if she'd been chewing on her mother's cotton balls. She couldn't have spoken if her life depended on it, but then no one seemed troubled by her stillness. They were lost in their own words.

"See you then," Phoebe said as she managed a half-hearted wave and turned to complete her journey alone. Phoebe stood for a moment to watch the two figures walking away from her as they grew smaller on the horizon. She couldn't move, and she couldn't speak, and she couldn't even cry. She just watched.

Waiting for her science class to begin the next day was worse than ever for Phoebe. She sat slumped at the lab table, tracing the raised letters on her yellow pencil with her finger over and over again.

Cricket dashed in as if she'd run all the way from home and sat down at the table, which the two girls now shared. Phoebe nodded reluctantly but parted with no words. Cricket just smiled in that way she had that made her eyes scrunch up, all but disappearing.

"Today, class," Mr Carmichael was speaking with his normal sense of strained urgency, "I expect you to outline your science projects so you can get started on them at once!"

Phoebe barely managed to open her workbook, looking for a project which would require minimal interaction with her new partner.

"Oh, Phoebe, you have a rabbit, don't you?" Cricket asked with a bit more innocence in her voice than necessary. Phoebe glared over the top of her glasses, and Cricket abandoned her line of questioning instantly. Both girls' memories darted back to the day that they used Phoebe's dear old doll to set up a pretend hospital. Thankfully, Wart could rely on the more mature Phoebe Buttanshaw to protect him from any similar fate.

"Look, here's a good one," Phoebe said, pointing to the drawings of plants and cheery looking sunshines. "We can study the effects of prolonged light on seedlings. I'll grow the plants and you can draw up the charts."

It seemed a perfect solution to Phoebe. She liked plants, and she would only have to see Cricket at school unlike many of the other teams who seemed to relish the opportunity to work together even during their precious free time outside the classroom.

Phoebe found herself selling the notion to Cricket who, surprisingly, thought it sounded like a great idea. This positive reaction caught Phoebe off guard and even lifted her mood slightly.

After school that day Phoebe didn't take her normal route home. Instead she visited the local garden centre where she lovingly selected her group of fragile little plants.

When she returned home Phoebe measure the height of each seedling and arranged a lamp above half of them. Working in the solitude of the family garage gave Phoebe a sense of peace, and she forgot for a few hours all about school and Cricket and science class and even about Kip O'Conner.

The next two weeks lipped quickly away as Phoebe tended her plants and tried to avoid Cricket Allison. She'd even altered her route to Fielder's School rather than take a chance on meeting Cricket who would insist on discussing science. Cricket Allison and science class! What a distasteful combination poor Phoebe found this.

Phoebe had to admit that she felt a smug satisfaction at the way she had managed to separate the responsibilities for the science project into two distinct camps with herself working in the happy solitude of the garage and Cricket drawing charts and tables somewhere, anywhere, else.

Friday was the day of the Fielder's Science Fair so Phoebe was up early, gathering her seedlings and packing her lamps and equipment. All the data had been passed onto Cricket who was constructing the accompanying posters.

It was a cool, sunny morning as Phoebe started her walk to school. She'd decided to revert to her favourite route again now that she'd survived the two week sentence with Cricket. Each brick and paving stone seemed to welcome her back as the sunlight bounced off of them, encouraging a skip in Phoebe's gait. The science project was all but at an end, and it would soon be time for the Spring break. All seemed to be improving in the world of Phoebe Buttanshaw.

Approaching the last turning before Fielder's School, Phoebe slowed her pace as she spied Cricket Allison waiting on the corner in front of her. She was sure that Cricket was hesitating in the hope of meeting up with her before delivering the project to the long main hall where the science fair was to be set up, and she felt just slightly unkind at delaying the inevitable meeting. With a heavy sigh of resignation, Phoebe decided that it might be best to simply get the job completed, and so the jaunt returned to her step; and she began a determined pace straight in Cricket's direction.

"Oh, great!" I've been waiting ages to see you!" Cricket's face lit up in Phoebe's direction.

Phoebe didn't speak but instead screwed up her face in a perplexed expression at the unabashed pleasure in Cricket's welcome. What could it mean?

Before she had time to ponder any hidden meaning in her old rival's greeting, Phoebe had her answer. From behind her ran an agile youngster with a face which glowed as much as Cricket's It was Kip O'Conner who carried under his left arm several poster-size pieces of white cardboard.

Phoebe felt that she'd perhaps become suddenly invisible as she watched from somewhere outside while her rival and her friend came together in swirls of warmth.

Slowly, Phoebe pieced together the puzzle as Kip handed to Cricket about half a dozen posters covered with big, clear letters explaining the effect of prolonged sunlight on developing seedlings. Each bit of information had been carefully illustrated with Kip's distinctive little funny characters, each representing the seedling in question. It was all very artistic and very clever so perhaps Phoebe should have felt happy at this unexpected contribution to the Buttanshaw/Allison science project, but she didn't.

Instead Phoebe felt jealous and ashamed and foolish and hurt. She was so jealous of the obvious hours that Kip had spent in helping Cricket with her part of the project that she was positive that if her clown mirror were handy at that very moment, those very clowns would be rolling with laughter at the sight of Phoebe's green face. And she was ashamed that she'd abandoned Cricket in what should have been a joint project between the two girls. And she felt extremely foolish that her childish refusal to work in union with Cricket had, in the end, left her out in the cold while throwing Cricket and Kip together in some strange alliance of science data and poster making. And Phoebe Buttanshaw was downright hurt to think that the boy who had, she was sure, become her one true friend had left her behind.

She stood looking at her toes for a long time. They seemed so very far away and rather unattached to her body, she thought. Finally Phoebe relented and walked towards her old school. School must go on. It always did, didn't it? Throughout her life, Fielder's School was always there whether Phoebe particularly welcomed it or not; and that day would be no different. She would go numbly up the long stairs and enter the great hall and join in the science fair. She would attend her day's classes and see the afternoon out, and only then would Phoebe Buttanshaw be free to rejoin Annie and Wart in the private sanctuary of her own little room where she could reflect on the day's events.

Phoebe Fall into Spring

Phoebe Buttanshaw had just discovered that she was a Pisces. Anyway, that's what the Sunday paper told her. It meant that she was kind and sensitive and tended to slip away into a dream often as not; but, more importantly to Phoebe, it meant that she would soon turn 14. Ever since that day last year when she had taken the giant leap into that great unknown call The Teen Years, Phoebe had looked forward eagerly to leaving the age of 13 behind her.

Being 13 has never been easy for anyone, but for Phoebe it just seemed to be one crisis after another. Perhaps starting a new year and being a new age would mean a new pattern emerging in Phoebe's life.

As she lay in her bed turning the possibilities over and over in her mind, Phoebe's attention came to rest upon the red notebook laying on the bookshelf where it had been carelessly tossed last autumn and where it had remained, all but forgotten, until that moment.

It was Phoebe's business records. She had begun her neighbourhood lawn mowing service on her 13th birthday. Suddenly, with her 14th birthday speeding toward her Phoebe realised that it was time to reacquaint herself with those lawns which she'd loved so well just last year.

Phoebe jumped from the warmth of the pink bed and pushed birthday thoughts from her head. She didn't even give a glance into the clown mirror's direction as she dashed toward the window. The daffodils had returned! When had it happened? In the night? Or had it been while she sat with curtains drawn contemplating life and Kip O'Conner? Could she really have come so close to missing the arrival of her beloved spring?

Phoebe pulled on her work clothes and then flung open the closet door. Her eyes quickly scanned the row of carefully arranged shoes. There were weekday school shoes, Sunday dress-up shoes, long-forgotten dancing shoes, but not a single pair of adequate lawn mowing shoes. This would definitely mean a visit to the nearest shoe shop, but for now Phoebe would have to make do with her green Wellington boots. So, with feet clad only in thick white cotton socks, Phoebe raced toward the stairs and the back hallway where the Wellies lived.

Out the bedroom door towards the top step she ran, skipping from step to step as she'd done as long as she could remember. That's when something went terribly wrong. Did she misjudge her footing? Did the cotton socks slip on the worn carpet? Or was it merely the grand finale in a series of 13-year old mishaps?

Phoebe's thoughts seemed to be in tune with the slow motion of her awkward movements as her feet flew up into the air, and her back hit the stairs. She bumped along, bouncing ungracefully from step to step until finally she rested at the bottom in an unsightly heap.

Instantly Mrs Buttanshaw appeared from nowhere as mothers do in such emergencies.

"Oh, Button!" The look in her eyes was that of a terrified parent who was trying to give an outward appearance of calm.

Phoebe thought she must be in shock, for she felt no pain at all. In order to prove that no damage had been done, she jumped nimbly to her feet only to collapse immediately. That was when Phoebe felt the pain for the first time. It shot through her foot and into her ankle like a flaming arrow.

Mrs Buttanshaw wrapped Phoebe in the arms of a mother's love and with strength known by those who are forced to act in such an emergency, she hoisted her daughter high into the air and carried her to the car outside.

The two spent that afternoon in the casualty ward at the local hospital. It seemed like hours before Phoebe's name was called and, as she waited, Phoebe watched glumly as her left ankle grew and grew until it looked as if it should be on an elephant. Phoebe was sure she must be delirious as her thoughts kept returning to her Latin teacher, Mrs Lafayette, who had no ankles at all. Would Phoebe be permanently without a left ankle?

Eventually, Phoebe was examined and re-examined. She was x-rayed in many positions from many angles. All in all, she found it rather interesting until the announcement was made that Phoebe had, indeed, fractured a small bone in her left ankle. She sat up very straight in her wheelchair awaiting the verdict. Then she heard the fateful words, "You'll be in a plaster cast for six weeks."

"Oh, no!" Phoebe turned bright red. "That's impossible! You see, I mow lawns, and it's March now, and I couldn't possibly...." But Phoebe found herself being wheeled briskly down the hall as she protested.

Even as she was stretched out on the table Phoebe continued to believe that she could simply refuse treatment. And so, as Phoebe continued her verbal assault on anyone near enough to hear, she was suddenly taken in hand by a large woman wearing a big plastic apron who began to cover Phoebe's left leg in warm, gooey plaster. Slowly Phoebe gave up the fight and even found herself thinking that the warmth of the plaster was soothing on her poor injured limb.

Soon enough she was back in her wheelchair, plastered and defeated. As Mrs Buttanshaw received instruction on how to treat the broken Phoebe, thoughts of a long ago game of hospital entered the girl's consciousness, and she pictured poor Annie rendered armless by a mad goblin called Cricket who laughed and laughed until her eyes were nothing but mere slits.

It wasn't until the doctor presented her with her very own crutches that Phoebe returned to the reality of the moment. And it wasn't until she tried to stand with the support of those crutches that Phoebe's eyes filled with tears for the first time. She had never really prided herself on her co-ordination, so to move about on these metal sticks was going to be a real challenge to Phoebe, and, besides, it hurt. It really hurt.

It was pure relief for Phoebe to be back in her snug little bed where such a brief time ago she'd been making plans to renew her beloved outdoor activities. Life sure was funny. If Phoebe Buttanshaw had learned nothing else in her 13 years, she had learned that life was very funny.

There were only two days of classes left before the mid-term break, so Phoebe would miss little in way of schooling. Just my luck, she thought as she turned the pages of her red notebook.

Mrs Buttanshaw visited the school the next day to collect Phoebe's homework and to inform the teachers of her daughter's condition.

By late afternoon it was a completely miserable Phoebe Buttanshaw who sprawled on the big sofa watching a silent television. Who would have known that daytime television was so boring?

When the doorbell chimed, Phoebe jumped and then let out a little screech from the pain. The sound of the doorbell had cut through the stillness of the empty house and startled her out of her trancelike state. The immediate problem at hand was how to respond to the bell. Should she just ignore it? Phoebe didn't ponder long to decide that this was the sensible avenue to take, given the circumstances. However, the repetition of the bell's ring made it all but impossible for her to return to the somewhat limited comfort of her trance so Phoebe decided to try the crutches.

The distance between the sofa and the door seemed to grow with each step she managed. Surely, that wouldn't be possible, and yet it appeared to be happening. Finally, Phoebe's fingers touched the handle of the door, and she even managed to pull it towards her enough to reveal the majority of the O'Conner family huddled on the doorstep.

There was Ollie O'Conner who looked as if he'd recently enjoyed the delights of a large bar of dark chocolate, and next to him was the always-smiling Augie, and behind him stood Kip O'Conner who surely must have grown two inches since Phoebe had last seen him! The sight of this trio wouldn't have warmed everybody's heart, but it was just what Phoebe needed most at that moment, and she felt a slight mist invade her eyes.

Kip looked at Phoebe for a long moment with a concern that she hadn't seen before. It was all too much, and Phoebe had to turn away. By then Ollie and Augie had made themselves quite at home in front of the television. Finally Kip jumped across the threshold, pulling from behind his back three perfect daffodils. Phoebe gladly accepted the yellow flowers, but, as she pushed the door shut, she couldn't help but glance at the long row of daffodils, which encircled her own front garden.

Kip clasped his arm round Phoebe's shoulder, helping her to the sofa, and she was surprised at the strength it possessed.

Once they had all settled, Kip disclosed the motive of this surprise visit. He had seen Mrs Buttanshaw at Fielder's School, and that's how he had learned of Phoebe's terrible accident. And so, here he was! He was going to take over Phoebe's lawn business until she was back on her feet. She could handle the books and phone contacts, and he would do the physical work. Ollie even said that he would help.

"What do you think?" Kip asked, full of smiles.

Phoebe couldn't think at all. She was overwhelmed. She would keep her customers and she would return to the job when she was mended and, best of all, she and Kip would be a partnership!

As an afterthought, Kip added that he'd mentioned the situation to Cricket Allison, and she'd like to lend a helping hand as well. Kip said that it would be a real team effort, but by then Phoebe's brain felt a little like mush. Maybe it was because she wasn't really a very nice girl or maybe just because she didn't understand or maybe just because she was 13 years old, but Phoebe Buttanshaw just did not want to be a part of any team that boasted Cricket Allison as a member. And yet, at the same time, she knew that if she refused to join that team, it wouldn't be Cricket who remained on the sidelines, and so Phoebe tried to force a smile from her silent lips.

The week that followed found Phoebe doing what she did best.....organising. She contacted all of her clients from the previous season, arranging dates and times for their first gardening session. Then she confirmed Kip's availability, and then she followed up with her customers, making sure that everyone was happy.

Things seemed to progress well through the first week of the Spring break. It was nice to have 10 full days without once conjugating a Latin verb or worrying about the wellbeing of the lab mice. And Phoebe's leg caused her less pain with each day.

Toward the end of the week Phoebe felt it might be time to try a walk down Elm Road to visit Kip at work on the Fulham's garden.

Mrs Fulham had been Phoebe's babysitter when Phoebe was four years old and Mrs Fulham herself was 14. Now Mrs Fulham was the mother of a four year-old daughter, and Phoebe occasionally acted as her babysitter. Once again she found herself thinking, life is funny.

Slowly making her way along Elm Road, Phoebe found the walk to be more exhausting than any gardening work she'd ever undertaken. Finally she was welcomed by the agitated yipping of Augie who followed the lawnmower up and down each strip of fresh cut grass, nipping at the wheels all the way.

When Kip noticed the exhausted face of the girl on crutches, he went to her and offered his arm for support. Phoebe was relieved to sit on the wooden bench as she wondered how she would ever make it home.

While Phoebe tried to catch her breath, Kip chased Augie around the open garden. Then he did what Phoebe thought to be a very odd thing. He stood for a long moment in silent concentration before leaping forwards onto the palms of his hands. Then his feet lifted into the air high over his head, and he walked on his hands the complete length of the Fulham's garden! This spontaneous performance thrilled Augie greatly, and he danced on his hind legs behind his master.

Phoebe's eyes were wide when Kip finally turned the right way around again. He gave her just the briefest of glances and said, "I helped out in a circus once."

Phoebe believed that he probably did. She believed whatever Kip O'Conner said because she had figured him out early on, and, although he was a genius at fabricating far-fetched tales for whomever else might listen, Kip had never misled Phoebe. Never……and Phoebe had confidence that he never would. This arrangement made her feel that she had a special status where Kip was concerned, and she liked that.

Phoebe sat under the branches of the oak tree and studied the buds carefully. It wouldn't be long before the green returned to the trees in united declaration that life goes on and on. She loved the spring. As Phoebe remained deep in her thoughts and Kip remained deep in his work and Augie remained deep in his slumber under a lawn chair, another presence made itself known.

"Lunchtime!"

It was the overly cheerful Cricket Allison carrying a woven basket and wearing what had to be the first pair of shorts of the spring season. She ignored Phoebe and Augie, making a beeline for Kip.

"Oh, you need a break. You've been working so hard."

Phoebe couldn't take her eyes off this girl who hadn't seemed to grow taller for years. She was wondering whether Cricket's hair ever grew either, as it had been the same short style forever. Could it all be due to some exotic vitamin deficiency? As Phoebe watched, Cricket waved a checked cloth into the air and then spread it out onto a sunny patch of the lawn. Busily arranging sandwiches and snacks into neat little rows, Cricket finally looked in Phoebe's direction.

"Oh, hi, Phoebe. I'm sorry but I didn't expect to see you so I haven't brought you any sandwiches." It was odd, but Phoebe's appetite had suddenly vanished anyway. She would have liked very much to have run home at that very instant, but she couldn't move let alone run. Instead she sat and watched as Kip and Cricket shared lunch and jokes.

Phoebe couldn't yet put her finger on it but there was something mysterious about the way they communicated. Cricket watched Kip's face too intently, laughed slightly too long at his jokes, and was just that bit too eager to be helpful around him. Why didn't Kip see it, she wondered. And, although Kip gave Phoebe his honesty and his concern and shared her love of angels and dogs, he didn't look at her the way he looked at Cricket.

While this truth tore through Phoebe's mind like a bolt of lightning, her hand moved without thought to her glasses, and she pulled them from her face. Phoebe couldn't explain what she felt. It was something new and unfamiliar. It wasn't what she'd felt at age 10 when she'd just made friends with the new girl at school only to find that she had to move away again, and it wasn't what she'd felt when she'd wanted so badly to win the spelling bee at school but the prize went instead to Lenora Lindermost. She recognised the feeling as a hurtful one, but different at the same time. What could it mean? How long would it last? Would it ever go away? Or was it all just an upset tummy from last night's spicy chilli? Phoebe was full of questions but had few answers.

Slowly, painfully, she rose to her feet and inched her way toward the garden gate. For just an instant, Phoebe's eyes met Kip's, but Phoebe quickly lowered hers in an act of self-survival as she said farewell to the two picnickers. Only once did she dare look back over her shoulder. Cricket was turned away from her, but Phoebe could see that her head was thrown back in animated laughter. Kip's face, however, showed something else. It only added to Phoebe's confusion, for Kip wore the same expression worn by herself. It was impossible for Phoebe to imagine Kip O'Conner to be anything other than confident and self-assured, but perhaps just this once he was actually sharing Phoebe's feelings of bewilderment.

With a heavy sigh and a nudge at the spectacles, which had been returned to their rightful place, Phoebe somehow managed to return home. Mrs Buttanshaw had to help her exhausted daughter into bed, tucking her in very tightly as if to protect her from the woes of the world.

Before her mother turned to go, Phoebe found herself giving in to the uncontrollable urge to throw herself onto Mrs Buttanshaw's shoulder. The tears found their way into each crevice of the loving mother's neck as she held her quivering daughter.

Phoebe wished and wished that she could be 3 years old again or even 30 years old …. Anything but 13.

"14"

Phoebe Buttanshaw was famous for her impatience. There were moments when she felt as if she'd simply burst apart if her life didn't just kick itself into high gear. Many times she felt that she absolutely could not wait one minute longer for ….. well …. For something, and even Phoebe Buttanshaw, herself, hadn't the slightest idea of what that something might be.

On this particular day Phoebe was anxious for two very real eventualities. She was eager to have her plaster cast removed, and she was more than ready to become the golden age of 14. She was still weeks away from any hope of escape from the plaster, but the day for celebrating Phoebe's 14 years was merely one day away.

The thought of it lifted her spirits as she pulled herself from her bed. Balancing on one unsteady leg, Phoebe teetered precariously as she stretched to reach the pencil lying atop the chest of drawers. Although it tried very hard to avoid her grasping fingers, in the end it succumbed, and Phoebe held the yellow stick for a moment before pushing it firmly into the space between the plaster and her wounded leg.

The relentless itching could not be combated, but Phoebe was determined to try and, so far, the yellow pencil was the best weapon she'd found against the nagging problem. Mrs Buttanshaw had tried to comfort Phoebe by saying that the itch was really a very good thing, for it meant that her poor leg was on the mend. Somehow, though, Phoebe found the words hollow and only viewed the itch as insult added to injury.

After many unsuccessful attempts to reach the annoying itch, Phoebe looked at the pencil and remembered what she was supposed to be using it for. Falling back against her favourite comfy pillow, Phoebe picked up a pad of lined paper and looked at the blank page. The homework assignment called for her to write an essay entitled 'In 10 Years I Will Be....' Phoebe held the pencil close to the paper and willed it to begin the work at hand. She felt little surprise when there was no response.

Phoebe found her mind drifting into a daydream as she tried to envision herself as a fully grown adult person. What would become of her? There was a time when she thought that she could picture herself as a famous actress, admired by one and all. However, since the Camelot catastrophe, Phoebe had abandoned any such ambition. Perhaps veterinary medicine would be her calling. But, being realistic, Phoebe knew that she would never be able to plod through years of science courses that a medical degree would require. Would she become a renowned novelist? Looking at her blank paper and the pencil, which refused to follow her demands, Phoebe somehow doubted it.

The more Phoebe searched for answers, the more exhausted she became until her body finally gave up the fight and sleep overtook her.

Dreams darted in and out of Phoebe's sleep like channels on a television set. In each of her dreams, Phoebe had two healthy legs. She knew this because she kept finding herself being chased by crazed rabbits or roller skating down railway tracks or numerous other far-fetched scenarios.

At one point, Phoebe felt herself flying high above the treetops next to a winged Shu-Shu, and she felt happy to see Shu-Shu looking so well. Phoebe had always loved the flying dreams best, and this one was no exception until, that is, she glanced below only to see Kip O'Conner and Cricket Allison still enjoying the picnic on the checked tablecloth.

That is when a loud tapping on the bedroom door startled a thankful Phoebe from her slumber. In burst Aunt Sue who never missed a chance to spoil her favourite niece with unusual gifts of dubious taste. Her very first gift ever to Phoebe had been the clown mirror presented on the day of Phoebe's birth nearly 14 years earlier. Throughout the following years Aunt Sue had proudly presented a string of odd presents including a clock in the shape of a black cat whose eyes and tail moved from left to right with each tick, a pink sweatshirt with purple rhinestones spelling out the words 'I'm Cute', and a huge potted plant made out of multi-coloured feathers.

As soon as Phoebe became old enough to voice an opinion, Aunt Sue's gifts seemed to find themselves banished to the back corner of the cupboard where they hid in embarrassed isolation.

"Happy birthday to my favourite niece!" said a big voice escaping from a big woman. "And how's that poor little leg?"

Aunt Sue didn't wait for a reply but decided instead to get right to the point of her visit. "Wait until you see what I've bought for you! I saw this in the shop and just knew that it would be perfect for my little Buttons!"

Phoebe eyed the brightly wrapped package with some caution before taking it into her hands and saying, "Thank you, Auntie Sue. I think I'll keep it until tomorrow if you don't mind terribly."

As Phoebe placed the present on top of the chest of drawers, she couldn't help but feel just a little guilty at her lack of enthusiasm although Aunt Sue didn't seem to notice it at all as she continued her jolly banter.

Aunt Sue was Mrs Buttanshw's only sister, and Phoebe had tried unsuccessfully many times to picture the two as youngsters growing up in the same household. In the end she gave up, deciding that there were simply some people who must never have been children at all as odd as that might seem.

The non-stop conversation with her Auntie Sue, although unexpected and even uninvited, did somehow seem to make Phoebe smile, and she even agreed to make the trek down the stairs for a family evening around the old kitchen table.

"So, what kind of birthday party have you planned, dear?" It was Aunt Sue's first comment as the Buttanshaws settled into their regular places for dinner.

"Oh, no!" Phoebe felt her cheeks redden. "I'm not having a party at all. No, no, definitely no party."

What with her leg in plaster and the image of Kip sharing a friendly picnic with Cricket still fresh in her mind, Phoebe was in no partying mood.

Phoebe lowered her head and stared into her lap for a long, silent moment. The subject was closed, and further discussion would only send Phoebe running back to the solace of her own room. The family seemed to accept this, and the subject of conversation soon jumped from topic to topic which relieved the nearly 14 year-old Phoebe Buttanshaw no end.

That evening Phoebe was back at her notebook, once again facing the task of completing the sentence 'In 10 Years I Will Be…..' She didn't know why it should be so complicated or why it should be that she felt more and more uneasy the longer she contemplated it. Somehow there just didn't seem to be an answer, and Phoebe drifted off to sleep with the untouched pad of paper still in her hand.

"Happy birthday to you, happy birthday to you, happy birthday, dear Buttons! Happy birthday to you!"

Phoebe opened one eye and squinted into the morning sunlight. She knew before taking that little peek that her mother would be standing over her bed, eager to be the first to acknowledge this special day.

Every birthday of Phoebe's life had begun this way with Mrs Buttanshaw singing the traditional birthday song and presenting the traditional birthday cake. Phoebe pulled herself up onto one elbow and eyed this year's confectionary offering. She had to admit that it was an amazing sight and wasn't really like a traditional birthday cake at all. Before her sat a lopsided mass of icing in the shape of a rabbit. At least Phoebe thought it must be a rabbit. The deduction came as much from the universally accepted knowledge of her love for rabbits as from any visual hint. Anyway, it was white with a round tail and two pink eyes and one and a half long ears. Phoebe couldn't imagine where the other half an ear had gone.

"It's perfect," she said to the beaming Mrs Buttanshaw, who suddenly looked extremely pleased.

With the morning sun of early spring shining on her cheeks she was really very pretty, Phoebe thought as she looked at her mother's sweet face. She decided right then that she really must try to have more patience with her especially now that she was 14.

Phoebe had a feeling that this day – this 5,114th day of her life – this 14th birthday – was going to be a very good day, and Phoebe was very intuitive. So, trusting her instincts, she rose from her bed and pulled on her very favourite green sweater.

She'd recently decided that green was a good colour in general and a very good colour for her in particular. Green was, after all, the colour of life as every tree knew, and it was the colour of Phoebe's eyes so wearing the green sweater always made her feel hopeful and, well, if she'd allow herself to think it, sort of pretty.

Mrs Buttanshaw carried the rabbit cake downstairs and placed it in the centre of the big pine table as Phoebe slowly made her way to the kitchen until she finally reached her old familiar chair. Sitting there, holding a warm mug in her hands, Phoebe felt that her cares were miles away.

CRASH! Phoebe nearly fell off her chair at the loud noise coming from the back garden.

"Oh dear," Mrs Buttanshaw stood and looked mysteriously at the back door and then nervously at Phoebe. "I think it's Ollie O'Conner. He asked if he could feed Wart today, and I thought it would be okay."

With that she ran out the door leaving Phoebe hanging half on her chair and half on the floor. It seemed a bit of an over-reaction, Phoebe thought, but the Buttanshaws weren't known for their calmness.

Phoebe was curious but not curious enough to leave the comfort of her cup of tea. Anyway, she trusted Ollie and thought it was sweet that he wanted to feed Wart for her. She was sure that the source of the noise would prove to be innocent.

Eventually Mrs Buttanshaw returned and looked at Phoebe with an odd, expectant expression and a glazed, fixed smile.

"Yes?" Phoebe remembered her earlier silent promise of patience, but really, she was already finding it difficult.

"Phoebe, dear, would you come with me please?"

Phoebe's curiosity now outweighed the attraction of her warm drink, and she rose unsteadily. Rearranging her crutches until they were in their most comfortable, uncomfortable position, Phoebe inched herself toward the back door.

Mrs Buttanshaw pushed the door open wide for Phoebe, inviting in the flood of March sunshine. The sudden glare made it difficult for Phoebe to see, and she blinked several times before she could focus her eyes.

Ollie was standing there holding Wart close to his chest just as she'd expected. But Kip was there too. He stood at the side of a wooden table, which had been decorated around all the edges with big red balloons, and each red balloon had been decorated with Kip's funny drawings of a girl wearing round tin glasses. Banners shouting HAPPY BIRTHDAY hung from the trees and walls. Yellow daffodils filled vases on every surface. In the centre of the table sat a big wicker basket, which was open wide, and Phoebe could see stacks of sandwiches and treats.

"I thought it was a nice day for a picnic," Kip spoke directly to Phoebe.

She didn't know what to say. She just moved ever so slowly toward the table and touched the vase and then the balloons and then the lovely basket. It was just as she reached the basket that it caught her eye. It was cleverly buried under the sandwiches, but very little could get by Phoebe Buttanshaw especially on a day such as that one.

Still silent, she dug deep into the basket and pulled out a square package. It was wrapped but not in traditional wrapping paper. Instead it was covered in plain brown paper, which had been decorated by hand with drawings of red balloons and yellow daffodils. Phoebe was intrigued but remained speechless.

Kip nodded in the direction of the present, which Phoebe took as an invitation to unwrap it, and so she did. As the brown paper fell away, a shiny white gift box was revealed. It had the words 'Over the Moon' inscribed in golden letters. Phoebe's heart skipped a beat. She pulled open the lid and saw the white tissue paper, which was covered in pictures of a cow jumping over the moon. Carefully, she removed the tissue. It was all so beautiful!

Most beautiful of all was the wooden carved jewellery box, which Phoebe held in her hands. She loved it.

"Open it, silly," Kip laughed.

Only then did Phoebe realise that it was a musical jewellery box, but a very special one for where one usually expects to find a ballerina spinning to the tinkling sounds, this perfect box held a snow white angel who turned round and round gracefully.

Phoebe was unable to speak throughout most of the picnic brunch, but that had never been a problem for her and Kip, and Phoebe knew that they shared something very precious and rare. And so they enjoyed their sandwiches, and then they enjoyed the rabbit cake, which was shared by Ollie and Mrs Buttanshaw.

That evening Phoebe sat in her room and thought about that special day. Her intuitions had told her that it would be a good day, and indeed it had been.

As she turned the pink blanket back and fell clumsily onto the bed, Phoebe spied Aunt Sue's present, lonely and unwrapped, atop the chest of drawers. She felt suddenly very naughty for having ignored it all day, and so she lifted herself up and stood shakily. Leaning against the chest of drawers to steady herself, Phoebe pulled the shiny wrapping from the gift. She wondered if this, too, would be delegated to the cupboard along with the feather plant and the cat clock.

Surprise swept over Phoebe as she looked at the unwrapped present. She held it in front of her and thought, Aunt Sue is full of surprised. Then Phoebe looked at the clown mirror, which Aunt Sue had given her all those years earlier.

Her fingers touched the carved clowns, and Phoebe lifted them from the spot on the wall where they'd lived for exactly 14 years. She turned to the cupboard door and opened it. For one lingering moment Phoebe held onto the pink and yellow clowns as she was flooded by memories from the past 14 years, all of which were somehow tangled up with those gentle characters dancing around the frame of that mirror. Then, with one brisk movement, she tossed the mirror into the back of the cupboard and turned again to Aunt Sue's new present.

Phoebe couldn't have selected a more perfect, grown-up mirror herself. It had finely bevelled edges and was framed by a lovely piece of wide antique pine, which had been hand-finished in a subdued stain. She placed it on the same nail, which had held up the clowns securely for many years.

Gazing at the girl reflected in the glass, Phoebe thought that she had travelled a long way since the early days of the clowns, and she wondered how it was that life could be so simple and so complicated at the same time.

After many minutes had passed, Phoebe picked up the notepad, which was still laying on the cluttered chest of drawers just below the new pine mirror. Hastily she scrawled, 'In 10 years I will be…..24 years old.'

Who is Jane Quinn?

Jane Quinn is the author of this book. Just like Phoebe Buttanshaw, Jane turned thirteen years of age once. She remembers it well as it was the year she started her writing career. Since that date she has interviewed and photographed hundreds of Pop and Rock stars for books and magazines. She loves Cairn Terriers and Scottie dogs and her strange husband Tim. Originally from Fishers, Indiana, Jane now lives near Liverpool in England.

www.ingramcontent.com/pod-product-compliance
Ingram Content Group UK Ltd.
Pitfield, Milton Keynes, MK11 3LW, UK
UKHW020909070726
473031UK00001B/10